GAREN

SHIFTER ROMANTIC SUSPENSE

ANN GIMPEL

Edited by
ANGELA KELLY

Illustrated by
FIONA JAYDE

CONTENTS

GAREN

~

Rubicon International, Book One
by
Ann Gimpel
Undercover Shifter Bad Boys = Alphas With Serious Attitude

Tumble Across the Rubicon Into the Death-Riddled World of
International Espionage

THE BIRTH OF RUBICON INTERNATIONAL

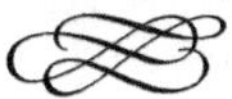

*C*rossing the Rubicon is an expression that means taking an irrevocable step, casting the dice, and being willing to live with the consequences.

Boston Harbor
September, 1773

"You can come out now."

Garen pounded a fist on the cabin Lars had barricaded himself into a few hours after their ship sailed out of Marseille's harbor four weeks before. They'd run into a spate of rough weather, or they'd have made Boston a week earlier.

Garen knocked again, louder this time although as a mountain cat shifter, Lars had exceptionally keen hearing.

"Stop!" Lars' heavily accented voice growled from beyond the door. Moments later, it flew open.

Garen fell back a pace. His friend was noticeably lighter, and his face held a haggard aspect. "Christ, you look like hell. I know you didn't leave your cabin much, but didn't the crew bring you food?"

A gurgling snort rippled past Lars' lips. "What for? I would just have heaved it back up. I ate, but not much."

Garen gazed about the cabin. "Looks like you're ready to leave."

Lars didn't answer. Just moved his collection of valises, crates, and leather bags toward the door. "I have been *ready to leave* for weeks. I will need a day or two to recover."

Privately, Garen thought he'd need longer than that, but shifters had decent recuperative powers. Much more efficient than their human counterparts.

"Where are your things?" Lars gathered his long, white-blonde hair in both hands and tied a leather thong around it, binding it into a thick queue that hung down his back.

"I hired a lackey. He'll be around any moment for your luggage. A carriage on the docks will take us into town."

Lars squeezed his gray eyes shut for a moment. "I cannot begin to describe how anxious I am to get off this ship." He dropped into shifter mind speech. *"Cats were never meant to travel over water."*

Garen punched him in the arm. "Maybe not."

"Remind me why you dragged us across the Atlantic."

Garen frowned. "Why? You already know."

"Humor me, old friend."

"Simple enough. The chaotic political environment in Europe and—" Garen switched to telepathy *"—that lucrative job offer spying for the newly formed American Colonies."*

"Thank you for indulging me. I needed to hear the *lucrative* part again. It does not exactly make up for how miserable I was, but—" Lars broke off abruptly when the shaggy, smelly man Garen had hired to transport their luggage trotted into view.

"These things?" He pointed at the collection of bags and raised rheumy, brown eyes to peer at Lars. "Rough for you, eh? Some folk, they never get sea legs."

Garen cleared his throat. "Sooner you get our things moved to the carriage, sooner you'll get paid."

"Yeah, yeah. You hired my back, not my tongue." The man blew out onion-saturated breath and loaded Lars' items onto a wheeled cart he dragged behind him. Greasy, dark hair hung around his face, and his clothing had more patches than original fabric. Despite the chill weather, he was barefoot.

Once he left, whistling a tuneless song, Lars leaned closer to Garen. "Apparently the New World has not treated everyone well."

"Neither did the one we left." Garen cast an appraising glance his way. "You weren't planning to stay on this side of the Atlantic. Did the ocean crossing change your mind?"

A ghost of a smile lightened Lars' even features, but didn't quite make it to his eyes. "I came along for the adventure aspect—and got a bit more than I bargained for."

"Will you go back to Germany?" Garen led the way around the ship's deck to a rickety gangplank.

"*Ja.* Not for many months, though."

"Maybe by then, they'll have invented a more stable ship."

"Ha! Very funny."

Garen extended an arm. "The black carriage is ours."

"If town is not far, we should walk for many reasons. It will give us information and allow us—or me—to recover faster."

"Good idea. Annoyed I didn't think of it first." Garen trotted to the carriage. He paid the lackey and gave more money to the driver with instructions to leave their things at Newport House.

Lars had already started off at a reasonably brisk pace, considering how beaten down he'd looked in his cabin. Garen ran to catch up. He eyed thick timber on both sides of the deeply rutted dirt track leading into Boston. His wolf was close to the surface. Anxious to run free after the claustrophobic ship.

"What would you think about—?"

"Not a good idea." Lars cut in, casting a sidelong glance his way.

"It is an obvious suggestion. I would love to take my other form, but for that we need night and a location farther from human habitation."

"No one looks twice at us throughout Europe," Garen pointed out.

"True enough, but until we understand the lay of things here, it pays to be careful. Our kind are hunted through the Ottoman Empire."

Breath puffed through Garen's teeth, making clouds in the chill air. Of the two of them, Lars was the cautious one, and the more levelheaded.

"We were late arriving," Lars continued. "You missed your assignation by at least three days."

"They'll find me." Garen felt confident his employers would know his ship had finally docked.

A musket ball whistled through the air, distressingly close. Cursing in German, Lars zigged and zagged a path into huge evergreens with Garen close behind. Arrows followed, along with more rifle fire and a bevy of outraged shouts.

"What the hell?" Garen ducked behind a thick tree bole, shoving thick black hair out of his eyes.

"Arrows must mean the native dwellers on this land are unhappy about something." Lars shook his head. "Perhaps sending the carriage away was a hasty decision."

Peering through tree branches, Garen noted that other foot traffic on the road hadn't cleared out. Perhaps such things were commonplace here. He twisted his face into a grimace. "It appears we overreacted."

"I came to the same conclusion." Lars flexed fingers with claws extruding from the ends. They vanished quickly, but his control over his animal form was usually better than that.

Garen snorted. "My wolf's not happy, either. Let's hurry into town. We're bound to make a mistake or two. Neither of us knows anything about the American Colonies."

"We must learn, and damned fast," Lars muttered.

"You're better?" Garen eyed him closely.

"Having your feet on ground that's not pitching, heaving, and rolling would make anyone *better*." Still grumbling, Lars plodded back toward the road.

Garen trailed after him, alert for whoever had fired shells and arrows into the center of a busy roadway. Maybe coming here had been a mistake. Regardless, the journey wasn't off to a particularly auspicious beginning. His normally optimistic side rose to the fore in spite of everything.

Things can only get better from here.

Lars shot a sour look his way. "I helped myself to your thoughts. While I hope you are correct, we must exercise caution."

Garen clapped him on the back. "Concentrate on finding our lodgings. Whiskey and women should improve both our outlooks."

Lars laughed. "My cock is in as bad a shape as my stomach. Did you find any likely wenches aboard the ship? At least you were out and about."

"No women. Nary a one. Obviously not on the crew, but not among the passengers, either."

"And here I was imagining you enjoying the hell out of yourself in your berth."

Garen waved his right hand in the air. "Madame Five Fingers got a workout."

"Our kind do not fall prey to human diseases. I am certain Boston hosts ladies for hire. Perhaps we can locate some who still retain vestiges of youth and enthusiasm."

"Speak for yourself." Garen jutted his chin skyward. "I'm so unutterably charming, women fall into my lap."

"I have noticed," Lars murmured in a wry undertone. "In that case, lure two and send the one you do not want my way."

Garen scanned the streets and turned right when he saw a sign for their hotel. It was far more modest than he expected, but so long as the rooms were clean and hot water plentiful for baths, it should be fine.

"Not exactly London or Paris or Heidelberg," Lars murmured, mirroring Garen's thoughts.

He shrugged. "It was where my employer suggested I stay. If we don't like it, we can look for something more commodious tomorrow."

Lars gripped Garen's arm, forcing him to halt. "Two possibilities, old friend. Either this is the best Boston has to offer, or your employer does not hold you in much esteem."

Garen started to bluster a reply, but thought better of it and clamped his jaws shut. Lars was correct. They went back too far for him to argue the point. If this whole American Colonies idea turned out to be a bust, they could always book return passage to Europe.

LARS WOKE to light streaming through his room's single, dirt-crusted window, pleased to be almost completely recovered from his weeks at sea. The woman who'd pleasured him the previous night was long gone. She'd been competent—and not overly chatty. Two plusses in his book. He and Garen had shared a passable meal in the establishment's rather run down dining room. At least the spirits were decent. A bit young and raw for his taste, but he'd had worse.

He rolled to a sit and reached for yesterday's clothes, then changed his mind. He rummaged through a valise for something clean. Surely the hotel had a laundry service of some kind. He'd ask over breakfast. Because he had time, he sent his cat senses spiraling wide. He found humans, dogs, cats, and a variety of wild animals in the surrounding woods. There was even a hint of a different type of magic. When he homed in on it, he sensed a perversion of witch energy. Were shifters here as well?

Surely his kind had found their way across the Atlantic. Perhaps not large cat shifters, but wolves like Garen or bears or coyotes or birds. He muffled a snort. Like as not, other cat shifters had made his same error, only realizing they made pathetically poor sailors once it was too late.

"It did not kill me," he mumbled. "I can cross the ocean again." Bending to secure his bootlaces, he added, "Next time, I will be better prepared. I fear this New World will not be all Garen hopes."

As if his thoughts drew his friend, a muted knock sounded on his door. Lars stood, walked to it, and turned the deadbolt.

"Ready for tea and breakfast?" Garen asked, smiling broadly.

Of a height with Lars, Garen stood several inches over six feet with a well-muscled build. Blue eyes augured into Lars, twinkling with merriment.

Lars nodded. "Breakfast would be welcome. Do you suppose they have the ability to wash our clothing?"

"Yes. I already asked. Bring what you want cleaned." Garen winked. "I made friends with some of the servants."

Lars elbowed him. "One of the things I have always admired about you is your cheerful attitude."

"Girl flesh helps that along."

Before Lars could mine for details about Garen's night, heavy footsteps clumped toward them. Garen spun to face the open doorway. Power shimmered about him, but only another magic wielder would've sensed it.

A tall, raw-boned man with unevenly trimmed red hair came into view. Leather garments clung to his frame. He narrowed shrewd green eyes at them. "Which of you is Mister LeRochefort?"

"That would be me." Garen squared his shoulders. "And you are?"

"Tom Smith."

The lie pinged off Lars' shifter senses. For whatever reason, the man wanted to hide his true name, but why?

Garen frowned. Obviously, he'd picked up on the falsehood too. "My associate and I—" he gestured at Lars "—were about to have breakfast. Would you care to join us?"

The man drew his brows into a thick line that met over the bridge of his nose. "Not quite my plan for the day."

Lars readied power of his own. Whoever this Tom Smith was, it appeared he wasn't on their side. "What exactly did you have in mind?" Lars cut in.

The man's gaze whipped to Lars. "Who the fuck are you?" he grated out.

"Mister LeRochefort's associate. He already told you that." Lars moved a step closer. The man was large, but he could take him—if it came to that.

"You didn't give me a name."

"Well, the one you gave us is false." Garen spoke up. "The way I measure things, we're about even. You hunted me down for a reason. What is it?"

"Don't matter what my name is. My people hired you." He sneered, displaying a mouthful of missing and decaying teeth. "You're coming with me."

Garen shook his head. "I'm a free agent. I don't have to do anything I don't choose to." He motioned to Lars before turning his attention back to the stranger. "Tell you what, *Mister Smith*, my associate and I are going to eat something. I know I suggested you join us, but I've changed my mind."

Lars understood. He tucked his money pouch into his jacket and shouldered past the man, keeping him at bay while Garen locked his room and pocketed the skeleton key. Though he was ready for the man to start throwing punches or draw the knife that hung from a waist sheath, neither happened. Anger streamed from him in waves, though. Clearly, he'd been given orders and attacking them outright wasn't on the menu—at least not yet.

Rather than going into the dining room, Garen moved on out the front door. "Let's see if we can find another option."

"How about over there?" Lars pointed across the street at a saloon that was clearly open despite the early hour. They'd have some type of food.

Garen nodded and pushed through swinging doors into a dark space that smelled like moldy beer. Sawdust was scattered across the floor. They found a corner table, ordered bread and cheese, and waited to see if their visitor would show up—with reinforcements.

Lars began eating as soon as a young girl brought their food. If he was any judge, they'd be on the run soon. Who knew when they'd have the luxury of eating again. Unless they switched to their animal forms and hunted.

"There's other magic here," Garen spoke into his mind.

"Yes. I sensed it too, but our friend back in the hotel was merely human."

"I can't believe Mister Smith—or whatever the fuck his name is—works for the people I corresponded with. It doesn't feel right."

"For once we are in agreement." Lars drained a tankard of terrible tasting ale.

"Have you had enough?"

Lars glanced at the empty plate. *"Nothing more to eat. What do you have in mind?"*

Garen got to his feet, leaving a few coins on the table. *"There's a stable to the south. I can smell the horses."*

"These places always have back doors off the kitchens. I say we locate it. It may buy us a few minutes grace."

Garen favored him with a toothy grin and switched to spoken words. "Funny, but I was about to suggest the same thing." He headed in the opposite direction from the front door.

Lars followed him. They'd discovered quite by accident that their animals' ability to converse telepathically extended to their human forms. Blood cemented that particular bond. Regardless, it was a handy skill.

After a terse exchange with a very annoyed cook after they invaded his small, filthy cooking area, they followed an alley until they hit the rear of a large stable. "I'll procure two horses," Garen told him.

"What about a wagon for our things?"

Garen twisted to face him. "Any idea how we can return to the hotel without tipping our hand?"

"I am certain someone is watching for us. If we do not emerge from the saloon soon, they will look more closely. If I were them, I would have a man posted near the stable." He pressed his lips into a thin line. "Our resources are far from infinite. We will need what we brought if we are to survive here."

"We'll play it your way." Garen nodded tersely. "I'd rather stand and fight than hide."

"This is Boston, not the western frontier. I do not believe anyone will take us on in broad daylight. Not until we have cleared this town's boundaries. Then all bets are off."

"Let's hope you're right."

Lars hoped he was too. While Garen dickered for horses and a wagon with a canvas cover to protect their things, he considered their next move. It made sense to remain near Boston. They needed work, and Boston was the primary staging area for the rebellion he suspected was imminent. It was only a matter of time before the Colonies waged out and out war to rid themselves of the yoke of British sovereignty.

The question of the hour was which side to align themselves with. Garen had already picked the Colonies. It made sense, but Lars wasn't totally convinced—yet. He rounded the corner of the stables and met Garen in front. He was still talking with the stableman, so Lars took a good, hard look at the two horses.

Both appeared sturdy, and neither flinched when he approached. Many horses were sensitive to shifters. Fortunately, not this pair. The wagon had seen better days, but the beaten metal around the wooden wheels wasn't too pitted.

Garen jumped onto the box and clucked to the horses. Lars

swung up next to him as they began to move slowly up the street toward Newport House. It only took half an hour to transfer their belongings. Lars worked on that, while Garen settled up with the innkeeper.

Lars felt edgy, ready for anything, but they were the only ones moving about the hotel. He joined Garen in time to hear the innkeeper ask, "Where might you two gentlemen be heading next?"

"Not certain," Garen mumbled and turned away.

"Surely you know which direction," the innkeeper inserted smoothly. "North? South?"

"We'll figure it out as we go," Garen called over a shoulder. He glanced at Lars once they were outside. "Do we have everything?"

Lars nodded. "It is one of the benefits of not being here long enough to unpack. How is our gold coin holding out?" He climbed onto the high box, waiting for Garen to join him.

"The horses and wagon set us back a bit." Garen checked the ropes securing the canvas before springing onto the wagon's seat. He chirruped to the horses, and they headed out of town at a trot. "Innkeeper seemed a little too interested in our destination."

"I thought the same. I have been considering what it means."

"Did you come up with anything?" Garen scowled.

"*Ja,* but you will not like it."

"Try me."

"We are very good at what we do, you and me," Lars began. "Much of the behind the scenes maneuvering around the American Colonies is taking place in England. Someone likely wanted to get you out of the way. Make certain you were not available to spy for the other side."

Garen laughed uncomfortably. "I'm not that competent for them to go to all this trouble."

"All what trouble?" Lars furled his brows. "We paid for our own passage. Likely once we were here, without our usual complement of comrades, whoever has it in for you figured they could pick you off easily." He paused. "What they did not bargain for was that you would bring me along."

"I'm having trouble seeing either of us as that important."

Lars shrugged. "Fine. You come up with an explanation then."

"I don't have one, but I do have an idea for what comes next."

"Oddly enough, so do I." Lars gestured. "You first."

"There's opportunity here, but I'm sick of answering to anyone."

Lars stifled a grin. Maybe, just maybe, Garen was going to suggest exactly what he'd been thinking. "Go on."

"I say we form our own troupe of spies. We certainly have enough experience. I'd prefer to limit our new enterprise to shifters, though."

Lars sucked in a startled breath. He hadn't considered that aspect, but it made sense. From many angles. Shifters were intensely loyal to one another, stronger than humans, healed far more quickly, and lived hundreds of years. Sometimes over a thousand.

"You're not saying anything," Garen observed.

"Because I had not considered the shifter angle."

"Does that mean you came to the same conclusion about creating our own organization?"

"It does, but I see one small problem."

"What's that?" Garen asked.

"I am far from certain there are any shifters on this side of the Atlantic—beyond you and me, that is."

"Easy enough." Garen glanced his way. "We import them from the Old Country."

"*Ja*, and we will not tell the cats about how difficult ocean crossings are." Lars smiled broadly just before his nostrils flared. Something didn't smell right.

He opened his mouth to tell Garen to move the team off the road when Garen said, "I sense it too. Shit! That didn't take long."

"Why would it?" Lars asked pragmatically. "The longer head start we had, the harder it would have been to find us." He leapt from the box before the wagon quit rolling. "Move the fight away from the horses," he shouted.

"I'll be there as soon as I tie them up," Garen shouted back. "No point in them running all the way back to the stable."

"I'm more worried about them getting shot," Lars countered and took off at a dead run, shifting as he went.

Garen shifted, heedless of his clothes ripping. He could collect his boots afterward. The rest didn't matter. Fighting in his animal form was logical. The wolf was stronger and faster. Bullets were an impediment, but muskets were notoriously difficult to aim, and his wolf could dodge most rifle fire.

Lars' mountain cat was a sleek, silvery color with charcoal eyes. Garen ran hard toward where he stood in an aspen thicket atop a small rise. It was a good location because it afforded them a three-hundred-sixty-degree view and some cover.

He scented the air, grateful for his wolf's augmented sensitivity. That odd magic tang he'd noted earlier was back in spades. Good he'd chosen his shifted form. Magic against magic made sense. He drew alongside Lars and stared at four black-robed men running toward them. Still a quarter mile away, they were closing fast.

"Are they priests?" Garen asked.

"Not from any religion I know about. They are not carting rifles, so they must feel confident their magic will prevail." He nudged Garen with his snout. *"This employer of yours. Did you tell them you were a shifter?"*

"Of course not." Garen smothered irritation. *"Give me credit for a little sense."* He tossed his power in a wide net and blew out a surprised breath. *"Son of a bitch. They're witches."*

"Same scent I caught back at the hotel. It took me a while to recognize it because it's odd. More smoke and cedar than normal."

"Agreed, but that's what they are. Maybe there're different varieties here. We burned most of the ones in Europe."

"They hung them here, but that is not important. At least so far, they believe they are tracking our wagon. While we have the element of surprise on our side, you circle from the right. I will take the left."

"Two each?"

"Ja. Zwei. Leave at least one alive so we can interrogate him."

"Let's wait to see what they have in mind." Garen paused. *"I'm not averse to killing them, but let's wait until they declare war on us."*

"They already have. While we are waiting for them to proclaim themselves, we should get into position."

Garen melted from the clearing, sticking to tree cover and scattering power to hide himself. His wolf loved the prospect of a good fight even more than he did in his human form, but he recognized the wisdom of not killing humans for sport.

The man in the lead halted precipitously and kicked his head back, snuffling. He raised both hands, and the other three halted next to him, fanned out in a row. Garen felt the zing of power and figured they were communicating with one another. He didn't know much about witchcraft. Magic wielders were notoriously insular, unwilling to join forces outside their particular brand of power.

He scanned the men, assessing his two targets. One was tall and thin, the other more muscular. All had beards and shaved heads. The air took on an electric quality, almost as if it danced to the witches' orders. Two turned toward Garen, the other two toward where Lars hid in dense undergrowth. Power flowed from their raised hands. It held compulsion that made Garen's skin crawl. Bright, sharp heat broke over him, and he understood he had to move now, while he still could. If he hesitated, the witches' magic would snare him.

Shaking off the urge to surrender to the witches—run right into their trap—he moved closer, preparing to spring. The first two men would be easy. The others much harder since they'd scarcely sit back while their companions were murdered.

A streak of silver landed atop one of the men. Lars and the witch crashed to the ground in a swirl of power, grunts, and shouts. Garen switched objectives fast. One of the men drew a lethal looking knife. Before he could shove it into Lars, Garen arced through the air and landed on him, driving him to his knees.

He snarled and snapped, sinking his teeth into the man's neck. Blood, hot and coppery, jetted from torn vessels, drenching his pelt with gore. Something landed on his back, and liquid fire raced up one side.

Goddammit. Obviously his victim wasn't the only one with a knife.

Lars punched into his human body and leapt on the man who'd stabbed Garen. Wrenching the knife from his hand, he plunged it into his chest, driving it deep.

The fourth man turned and ran for all he was worth. Garen gave chase, catching him easily. He threw himself over the man's back, paws on his shoulders, and held him on the ground with the weight of his body. The man writhed and cursed, but Garen held fast. It would've been easy to kill him, but they needed information and the other three were well past speech.

Lars raced to his side. "I have this one."

Garen wasn't so certain. He held his position until Lars hooked the man's arms behind his back and bound them with a leather thong. He straddled the man's ass and held a blade to the side of his throat.

Satisfied their prey wouldn't escape, Garen drew on his magic and shifted, still breathing hard. "Who sent you?" he rasped. His side burned, and he threaded healing power toward where the knife had sliced through skin and muscles.

The man remained silent.

"If you tell us, we may allow you to leave alive," Lars said.

Garen heard coercion beneath his words.

The other man laughed. "Not very fucking likely, mate."

A snort blew past Lars' lips. "Your courage is misplaced." Lars pressured the knife against the man's neck until a thin line of crimson formed, weeping droplets of blood. Magic hovered around him, urging the man beneath to give up his secrets.

"Your power's wasted on me," the man gritted. "Save your time and kill me. I'll never talk."

"Braver men than you have eaten those words." Lars switched to mind speech and added, *"Take your wolf form and start with his feet."* He'd meant the words for Garen, but a low whine of fear escaped his victim, and he bucked against Lars' hold.

Garen pulled the man's boots off before reaching for his wolf. *"What do you think?"* he asked Lars. *"One toe at a time? Or should I just bite the foot off at the ankle?"*

The man writhed beneath Lars. Fear rose from him in choking waves that smelled like carrion.

"It appears he can hear us," Lars observed.

"I noticed the same thing."

As soon as his wolf solidified, Garen struck fast, closing his powerful jaws over the man's big toe. Bone snapped, and more blood splattered him. He spat the digit into the dirt to the accompaniment of bellows of pain. Ever methodical, he went for the next toe in line. It joined its brother in the dirt.

The man's bellows shifted to howls. The acrid stench of urine burned Garen's sensitive nose, and he understood the man's bladder had released. In spite of everything, he remained stubbornly silent beyond his cries of pain.

"Keep going," Lars urged. *"We do not have all day."*

Garen bent his head. Before he could snap off a third toe, the man screamed. "Stop. No more. I'll tell you what you want. Just stop."

Garen sent his shifter magic auguring into the man, seeking truth. He found it and pushed back into his human body. "I asked you once," he snarled. "Who sent you?"

"I work for the British Colonial government." The man's voice was muffled since Lars still held him face down in the dirt.

"Let him up," Garen said.

Lars shrugged. "Why not? It is not as if he can run from us." He swung off the man's body and stood by Garen's side.

The man dragged himself to a sit and covered his mutilated foot with a hand. A jolt of magic turned the air iridescent.

"No matter how much power you summon, you'll never get those toes back," Garen muttered.

The man trained dark eyes on him. "All I want is to stop the bleeding. I'll never walk right again."

"I wouldn't complain. You're still alive." Garen jerked his chin downward. "Why do your masters want me dead?"

The man's eyes turned to slits. "I have no master beyond Gaia, goddess of the earth. Witches retain independence."

"Fine. Fine." Lars clamped his jaw into a terse line. "Why were you after us?"

"Two reasons. You're shifters, and you were hired by the rebels. We can't allow them to add magic to their bag of tricks."

Garen frowned. "We called on our animal forms today, but how else would you have known something like that?"

Despite a face glazed with pain, the man managed a supercilious half smile. "It's why the Brits use witches. We sense other magic wielders."

"Not in Europe, you do not," Lars put in.

"Right." The man nodded once, sharply. "We're stronger here."

"How?" Lars pressed.

"Native magic strengthened ours. The shamans like us. They shared their power."

"Is that how you intercepted our mind speech?" Garen asked.

"Yes." The man opened his mouth but shut it before anything else came out.

"Fascinating," Lars muttered. "How many others will come after us?"

The question seemed to stymie the man. He hesitated and finally said, "Not certain. The group I worked with is all dead but me. Mostly they don't tell us anything beyond our assignments."

Garen understood. It was the same way he ran operations. "Did you tell those you report to that we're shifters?"

The man shook his head. "Didn't get the chance. We weren't certain until we got close enough to scent your power."

With a muffled grunt of pain, the man pushed to his feet. "I don't know anything else." Truth pinged off his words.

"One last question," Lars said.

"Yeah?" the man eyed him warily and rolled his weight back from the balls of his feet.

"Are there others like us here?"

For a moment the man looked confused. "Other shifters?" At Lars' nod, he went on. "Not many, but they're here. It's part of Native magic. They become one with an animal's spirit and take on its form."

Garen digested the information while the man walked slowly toward the dirt track. A cacophony of howls told him coyotes had already found the three corpses and were feasting merrily. The man had been cooperative, but they couldn't let him live. Garen caught Lars' eye. They'd worked together long enough, words weren't necessary.

In a flurry of glistening light, Lars' mountain cat streaked toward the man. A single paw swipe knocked him to the ground before Lars severed the vessels in his neck. It was a clean death. As close to painless as possible. Another flash of light, and Lars was human again, trotting toward Garen's side.

He grimaced, shaking blood off himself. "The witch dealt fairly with us, but we had no choice. He would have told his masters—the ones he claimed not to have—what we are."

"No, we didn't have a choice," Garen agreed. "Not so sure about *dealing fairly*. He only ponied up the truth because we cornered him."

Lars laughed wryly. "When you get down to brass tacks, it is sometimes the only reason anyone lets go of the truth."

Since their ripped clothing wasn't worth collecting, Garen

crooked two fingers at Lars, and they headed for where they'd left the wagon and team.

"You are quiet," Lars observed. "Does your side hurt?"

"You too," Garen countered. "Where we come from, we're born shifters. It appears there's more than one route to joining with an animal bondmate."

"Your injury," Lars pressed.

"I'll live. I'm not bleeding anymore. Another few hours, and my wound should be healed."

The horses whickered nervously, put off by the stench of blood, and Garen cursed softly. He should've thought to wash it off. The countryside hosted myriad small creeks. His wolf would've licked himself off, but he wasn't inclined to do the same in his human form.

He glanced at Lars. "We need water, so we don't totally spook the horses."

Lars detoured to a stream and stepped into it, squatting to sluice muddy water over himself. Garen joined him. "You missed a spot."

Lars made a huffing noise, not unlike his cat. "I probably missed many spots, but it will have to do. Even though we left no witnesses, we should be gone from here before much longer."

A few more handfuls of water later, Garen slipped and slid over moss-covered rocks. By the time he reached the wagon, Lars was partially dressed. He handed a muddy towel to Garen.

"Thanks." He dried off and dug clothes out of one of his valises, dragging trousers over his legs and a shirt over his head. "We can find our boots between here and the dead witches."

"Mine are in the wagon." Lars cast a knowing look his way. "I removed them before I left."

"Well aren't you Mister Think Ahead," Garen sniped.

"Finish dressing. I will retrieve your boots." Lars took off at a lope. He was back so quickly, Garen hadn't finished untying the team.

~

ONCE THEY WERE UNDERWAY, Garen said, "At least this clarifies it was truly the revolutionaries who hired me. I'd begun to wonder. The British have resorted to counter-espionage more than once."

"It also appears they were not aware they hired one with power."

Garen grinned. "Yeah, leave it to the Brits to ferret that out."

Lars snapped the reins lightly, and the horses picked up their pace. "They are world-renowned spy-masters. Beyond that, today's encounter sheds light on something for me."

"What might that be?"

"I feared you might have chosen the wrong side in the battle that is sure to sweep through the Colonies soon."

Garen laughed. "Same thing occurred to me—until we figured out the witches worked for the Brits. I'd rather die than work for those bastards. Not keen on working for the revolutionaries either, though. They did a deucedly poor job of guarding information regarding my arrival." He straightened his shoulders. "Didn't we decide we weren't going to work for anyone but ourselves?"

"We did, but we have yet to flesh out the finer points. Where to?"

"Back to Boston, but not right away."

"Say more, old friend."

"Boston is fairly large. We were only easy to find since they knew what ship we'd be on, and I was dumb enough to stay where they told me to." Garen shook his head hard. "What the hell was I thinking?"

Lars tossed one hand in a typically Teutonic gesture. "Had I not been so racked with seasickness, I might have—"

Garen waved him to silence. "It doesn't matter. I believe we can enter Boston quietly enough, no one will bother us. After a few days elapse, that is."

"How will we spend that time?" Lars furled his blond brows.

"Thinking through our new business. Fleshing out the details. How else?"

Nodding thoughtfully, Lars said, "We need a name."

"Aren't most spy operations incognito?"

"We are breaking with tradition. Developing a solid framework. I say we need a name."

Garen mulled it over as the horses' hooves clopped through packed dirt and mud. Birds cawed overhead, and a light rain began to fall.

"Since we are not returning to Boston immediately, we should shelter beneath some trees. Soon it will rain harder, and I would welcome a meal. Killing is hungry work."

Clucking to the horses, Garen urged them away from the track and into the woods bordering both sides of it. "How about Rubicon?" he asked.

"Huh?" Lars turned his gray gaze on Garen as if he'd lost his mind. "You mean the river in Northern Italy?"

"The same."

"What about it? We are far from there."

"We'll name our venture Rubicon."

A slow smile warmed Lars' eyes until they smoldered like coals. "Perfect. Ancient Roman law forbade anyone crossing the Rubicon with a standing army and entering Italy. Julius Caesar thumbed his nose at the rule and marched his troops across—"

"—Against all hope and expectation, the Roman legions offered him fealty," Garen finished the tale.

"Nothing wrong with your history."

"Maybe the name will work as well for us as it did for him." Garen drew the horses to a halt and swung down, sheltering under a tree to get out of the worst of the rain.

Lars joined him. "A sound thing to hope for."

"Maybe so." Garen smiled crookedly. "What about the Native shamans who befriended the witches? Do we want to explore their power too—if they'll accept us?"

"The prudent path is to leave them alone," Lars said thoughtfully.

"Even though they also bond to animals, there will likely be no love lost between our two varieties of shifter magic."

Garen nodded slowly. "You're probably right. We should start with our own kind—and stick with them."

"Agreed. There is money in the spy game. Opportunity. It will take time for us to send for our associates in Europe, but Rubicon will be stronger if we build it slowly."

"I have another idea," Garen cut in. "Once we're more or less established here, I can run things on this side of the Atlantic—"

"And I can operate Rubicon in Europe. I like it." Lars made a sour face. "So long as I survive the next ocean crossing."

"I'll come along to make certain you do. And to help establish our presence in Europe." Garen paused, thinking. "Neither of us will be leaving for a few months. Winter's nearly here."

"True enough, and if my shifter senses see true, the Colonies will be embroiled in a full-scale rebellion sooner rather than later. We can make ourselves useful—to the revolutionaries. If we are astute, we will earn enough to give ourselves a foundation for future years." Lars moved deeper beneath a stout evergreen. "Heidelberg would make a most excellent European location for Rubicon. Centrally located. Easy to slip into other countries and back again."

"And you just happen to have a manor house there." Before Lars could offer more arguments, Garen added. "It's a solid choice. Much better than Paris or London or Berlin."

"I am moving off the topic, but I am hungry. We do not have any food, so—"

"Feel like a hunt?"

"Want to get the taste of toes out of your mouth, do you?"

Garen laughed and removed his clothes. Even if they only scared up field mice, they were a decent meal, so long as he caught several of them. "We can hammer out the fine points once our bellies are full."

"Good enough for me." Lars stuffed his folded clothing beneath the wagon's canvas covering.

"Ready?" At Lars' nod, Garen summoned power and let his wolf form take over. America was shaping up to be a grand adventure. He and Lars would create the toughest, most ingenuous spy company the world had ever known. It would be a success because they'd only train and hire shifters. Before things were done, they'd both be rich men. He knew it down to his bones.

Roll the clock forward a couple of centuries. Weapons have changed. Technology entered the scene, but espionage never fell out of fashion. Neither did the people who put their lives on the line keeping evil at bay.

As an agent for an international espionage firm, Miranda has her hands more than full. Between secretly lusting after her boss, Garen, and making sure the dirty little secret about her double life as a wolf shifter remains hidden, she's still a virgin at nearly thirty.

Sent to eliminate the head of a human trafficking organization in Amsterdam, she barely escapes with her life. Injured, frightened, and under attack the second her private jet lands in the U.S., she's not certain where to turn.

Garen's watched Miranda just as surreptitiously as she's been eyeing him. Unfortunately, the fact that she works for him is a showstopper. Plus, he has a few secrets of his own that have kept him single. When Miranda insists on heading up a covert operation, he can't come up with a plausible reason to stop her. Watching her sprint headlong into danger damn near kills him. He wants to hold her, love her, protect her.

Miranda's life is on the line. Will Garen risk exposure to save her?

CHAPTER 1

The Gulfstream G280 shuddered as it banked hard right. Miranda Miller pushed one of the window blinds out of the way. *Damn.* Black as pitch outside the aircraft. She felt like warmed-over crap. Her mouth tasted sour, and her eyes were hot and gritty. She rubbed them and tallied how long it had been since she'd slept. At least two days. She reached for a Styrofoam cup in its no-spill metal holder, sloshed cold coffee around her mouth, and swallowed.

Her headset hummed. "Wakey, wakey, *fraulein,*" a heavily accented German voice rumbled. "We land at JFK as soon as the tower clears us."

"What?" Fear sliced through her fatigue. "I told you we needed a smaller airport."

"Sorry, *fraulein.* This one was closest. We are below recommended minimums on fuel."

She considered asking the pilot why he hadn't planned better but decided not to antagonize him. It was bad enough they were flying without a copilot—probably against FAA regulations. She had a dummied-up commercial pilot's license tucked in her wallet under one of her many assumed names. Hopefully it matched the one on her phony passport. She hadn't had time to check. If it came down to it, she'd been instructed to tell the tower she copiloted the flight.

As if he'd read her thoughts, the pilot's next words were, "I need you to move into the cockpit, *fraulein*."

"Alrighty. Give me a minute."

"You do not have much more than that. I do not wish further difficulties with the U.S. authorities."

Miranda wondered just what other problems the pilot might be referring to. She almost asked him, and then decided she didn't really care. Her international security company engaged professionals. Most of them came from either the military or law enforcement and had checkered pasts. She unbuckled her seat belt and stumbled to her feet. Her crumpled, black pantsuit stank, but maybe only to her lycan senses. She hoped humans wouldn't be able to smell stale blood.

A muffled chortle made its way past her lips. Maybe once anyone got a whiff of days old sweat, they'd give her a wide berth. Her body ached, especially her ribs where her target had slammed a lead pipe into her. She fingered her side and wondered if anything was broken. Not much you could do for ribs. They had to mend on their own.

A few steps took her to the tiny head in the rear of the aircraft. She splashed cold water on her face and winced when she took a good look at her scraped knuckles. Her target in Amsterdam—head of a worldwide human trafficking organization—had been much harder to eliminate than she'd expected. She'd needed her supernatural speed and strength—and her wolf form. One more face-dunking in cold water and she grabbed a towel to dry herself.

"Now, *fraulein*." The jet shuddered again as its landing gear clicked into place.

The pilot sounded so exasperated, she rushed down the aisle and hurtled through the already-open cockpit door. He grabbed her arm and threw her into the empty seat.

"Watch it!" she snapped. Her upper lip pulled into a snarl. Claws pressed against the ends of her fingertips. Miranda struggled for control. Her wolf wanted to kill the human who'd manhandled her.

"Sorry." The pilot's voice was mild. She recognized compulsion beneath his words and wondered what the hell he was. "I do not wish to draw anyone's attention," he went on smoothly. "The rules regarding business-class jets are in constant flux." He glanced at her with gray eyes that didn't miss much. "Are you hurt?"

She nodded. "My assignment ran into unexpected snags."

"Will you require medical attention before you proceed to the West Coast?"

She snorted. What a subtle way of asking if she'd been shot or stabbed. Lars Kinsvogel—or whatever his name really was—had obviously dealt with people like her before. Something he said caught her attention. "Won't you be my pilot?"

He shook his head. "Someone fresh will relieve me."

"Will I be able to stay aboard?"

He shot her an odd look. "Of course not. You must go through customs."

She rolled her eyes and pressed her lips into a thin line. "That's why I wanted to land somewhere inland."

His gray eyes narrowed to slits. "All flights from foreign destinations are subject to customs, no matter what the airport. Is this your first international assignment?"

Heat rose to her face. "No." She was damned if she'd say anything else. She didn't know him from Adam.

The radio crackled. The pilot responded in pilotese and banked the plane. "Flights from Europe are cleared to land at certain airports. With the fuel we have left, we could have landed in Philadelphia or Newark, but I have a feeling those two destinations would not meet your needs, either. What are you afraid of?"

Miranda wasn't certain what she could tell him. Company policy was clear. Talk to no one. "Never mind."

She thought about Garen, her boss and chairman for Rubicon International. She'd been half in love with his razor-sharp mind, lithe build, salt-and-pepper hair, and sky-blue eyes for years, but he didn't see her as anything but a junior-grade agent. Rumor had it he scarcely acknowledged employees until they became full-fledged operatives. If her fellows were any indication, she had a way to go. At least a few more assignments. And then there was the problem of her being a lycan.

She sighed, and fantasies of Garen went up in smoke like they always did. It was nice to dream, but Miranda steered clear of men. Between her wolf side and her somewhat unorthodox career, intimate relationships carried too much risk of discovery. She relied on her fingers, a vibrator, and the occasional one-night stand to take the edge off her needs.

The jet banked yet again and dropped lower. Its wheels made contact, and the pilot hit the brakes. Because she wasn't belted in, Miranda nearly plunged into the instrument cluster. Lars made an aggravated clucking sound, but he didn't say anything. They taxied off the runway.

"Since I have to get off, I need to get my things together."

"Wait until the aircraft comes to a complete stop, *fraulein*."

He sounded so much like a bot, she stifled a laugh. The plane moved smoothly into an enclosed hangar. Once it rolled to a halt, she pushed out of her seat, returned to the passenger compartment, and unhooked her small duffel from the wall. Lars' breath hissed against her ear. "Where are your weapons?"

"On me and in my bag."

"Put everything in your bag. Clips separate."

"I'm not that stupid." She pulled a 9mm semiautomatic from its shoulder holster and punched the button to discharge its clip. She drew back the slide, extracted the chambered bullet, and stuffed it into the clip. Next came a snub-nosed .38 revolver and two knives. She spun the chamber to make certain all the bullets were out and then placed everything in locked gun cases in her carry-on.

Lars still stood practically on top of her. She met his gaze, noticing he was a few inches taller than her five feet eleven. "Yes?" She quirked a tired brow.

"Has anyone ever told you how beautiful you are?" He settled his hands on her shoulders. She smelled his arousal and knew he had a hard-on without even looking.

"Christ! Not now." She spun from beneath his grip. "Let's just get through customs and allow whoever's knocking to search the plane."

"We will have some downtime in the terminal. At least an hour." He sounded hopeful.

Miranda looked at him. Really looked at him. Lars was attractive in a Teutonic sort of way, with ice-blond hair and gray eyes. His trim body suggested he worked out. Interest flickered but then died. She shook her head. "I haven't slept for forty-eight hours. I'm dead on my feet."

"Why did you not sleep during the flight? The air was smooth."

Good question. She'd wondered the same thing. "I have no idea. Too keyed up, I guess."

He shouted something in German to whoever was pounding on the side of the jet and took her arm. "I will watch over you until you are safely back in the plane."

She opened her mouth to tell him it wasn't necessary, but something in his face stopped her. In that moment, she understood he was a trained operative just like her. His role this time around happened to be pilot, but she was certain he'd stood in her shoes before. "Which branch of the military trained you?"

He shook his head and let go of her arm. "It does not matter. Follow me, *fraulein*."

She shouldered her duffel and walked to the rear cabin door. Lars had just sprung the locks. He spoke soothingly in German to an obviously agitated customs officer standing at the top of the stairs. The agent's beady, black eyes settled on her. "Do you speak English?"

"Yes. Is there a problem, sir? It's been a long flight, and both of us are tired. It took me a while to get my bag together."

Nostrils flared, the agent looked intently at her and then stepped into the aircraft, waving them down the jet's steps. "Customs is the last door at the north end of the hangar," he barked. "Don't even think of running. This hangar is locked and fully alarmed."

Lars placed a hand beneath her elbow and guided her across a concrete floor. "It is best if we do not deviate from a straight line," he muttered.

"Holy crap," she said. "Why are they so uptight?"

He shrugged. "As you Americans say, it goes with the territory." He grinned, displaying very white, very even teeth. "Everything we do and say between here and the customs area is filmed and recorded."

Despite interested glances and furrowed foreheads, her munitions-heavy duffle passed inspection since her fake identification pegged her as an undercover agent for the Chicago Police Department. Miranda breathed a sigh of relief once they'd scanned her passport and released her. Even though Garen assured his operatives that each of their alternate credentials were fully covered at all ends, she'd never exactly believed Jayne Powers existed on the Chicago PD payroll.

They settled in a private lounge specifically for business-class jet crews and their passengers. At least an hour passed. Lars handed her a cup of coffee. He pulled a silver flask from an inner jacket pocket and waved it at her. Miranda shrugged. "Sure. I've never made a habit of drinking in the morning, but what the hell. What time is it, anyway?"

"Around five-thirty. It will be light soon."

She sipped the coffee, delighted to find he'd poured Irish whiskey into it. The liquor burned a path to her empty stomach. "Do I have time to grab some food?"

He frowned. "Probably. I do not understand why the relief pilot has not met us." He pulled a cell phone from his jacket and powered it on.

Miranda snapped upright from her slump against soft cushions. Deviations almost always meant trouble. She took one more slug of coffee and set her cup down. As tired as she was, she couldn't risk any more whiskey—not until she found out if something was truly amiss.

Lars punched in numbers, waited a few moments, and disconnected. He stood and held a hand to her. "We must go, *fraulein*." She opened her mouth to frame a question, but he shook his head. "We have stayed here too long, I fear."

She cocked her head at a restroom door near the rear of the private lounge. He nodded, obviously understanding her intent. If trouble was afoot, she needed to be armed. She went inside, ducked into a stall, and dug what she needed from her bag. The ammo clip slid into her 9mm with a satisfying *thunk*. She checked in a mirror to make certain her underarm holster was hidden. Her reflection shocked her. Gray circles etched beneath bloodshot blue eyes. Her dark hair hung halfway to her waist in greasy strands. She wound it into a queue and arranged it behind her shoulders.

Lars met her right outside the ladies' room. Miranda's practiced eyes noted the swell of a gun beneath his woolen jacket. She blinked hard to clear her head. Were they going to have a full-on shootout in the middle of JFK Airport? He shook his head almost imperceptibly, gripped her elbow, and propelled her into the corridor. At least this wing of the airport wasn't busy at this time of day. Only a few others strode meaningfully toward destinations.

He jerked his head sideways. A half-open door sat about fifty yards away. He bent so his mouth was right against her ear and whispered as they walked. "You will take the stairs all the way to the bottom. There is a door there. It opens into the main terminal. I will meet you if I can. If I do not, take a taxi. Put some miles between yourself and this airport." He made a sound somewhere between a snarl and a grunt. "Hell, if you can get the cabbie to drive you to the next state, do it."

She wanted to ask about finding a substitute route back to Seattle, but there wasn't time. He gave her a push, and the door snicked shut behind her. She heard it lock and understood he must've jimmied it somehow to get it open. She padded down a spiral metal staircase, grateful for her flat-soled, practical boots. Lights flashed whenever she passed a landing. She worried what to do if the door at the bottom was locked. She wasn't bad at picking locks, but she didn't have her pick set with her. She'd pretty much stopped carting it around because nearly every lock she'd run into in the last few years was electronic.

Don't borrow trouble. I'll find out soon enough.

Adrenaline twisted her stomach into a sour knot. Her wolf wanted out. It took precious energy to keep it contained. The stairs ended, and she stared at a metal door. The same blinking light flashed overhead. Wary of alarms, she twisted the handle. It didn't budge. *Shit!* She blew out a tense breath. Lars had managed to unlock the top one, so it couldn't be impossible.

She bent to examine the lock. The easiest thing would be to screw the silencer onto her gun and blow it to bits.

Yeah, right. Every cop in the joint will come on a dead run.

The lock had a card hole, which meant it was electronic. Maybe her lycan magic could tease it into compliance. She hummed a note, and then another. Something whirred at the edges of her sensitive hearing. The lock didn't give, not quite, but hope slammed into her. This could work if she was patient.

Miranda let a hand hover over the mechanism and felt its resonance. She tried a couple of three-note combinations. Her fourth try worked. She tamped down elation as the door popped open. She hurried through and tried to look casual as she tugged it closed behind her. Anxious to put as much distance as she could between her and the door—in case opening it triggered a silent alarm—she ran headlong into someone and muttered apologies before she realized it was Lars.

He pointed toward a glass revolving door. She stumbled after him. Questions bubbled around her tired brain, but she knew better than to talk on the cab ride. They got out in a neighborhood of stately old brownstones. Lars motioned her up several flights of steps and into an apartment furnished in Motel Six modern. He locked a series of deadbolts and turned to face her.

"Are we safe here?"

He nodded. "As safe as anywhere, *fraulein*, until I can get us out of the city tomorrow. I have made arrangements for a plane in Boston. We will fly to Seattle from there. Take the bedroom at the end of the hall. There is another bedroom, but I will sleep on the couch."

She raised a questioning eyebrow, but before she could formulate her question, he continued, "Normally, I would want to sleep much closer to such an attractive woman, but the couch is near the door in case we have…unexpected company."

Miranda was almost certain she knew the answer to her next question, but she asked anyway. "What happened to the other pilot?"

Lars curved his lips into a sneer. "Dead. The bastard who killed him will be too, once I get my hands on him."

Miranda walked down the hall and into the bedroom. She shut the door behind her, grateful Lars hadn't probed for details about her Amsterdam assignment. Human trafficking was global, but it still shocked her that the group she'd targeted had launched such an instantaneous retaliation. The relief pilot was dead because of her.

Stop! I can't think like that. He knew the risks when he signed on.

She shut her tired eyes, rubbing them. *Yeah, and so do I, but that doesn't mean I expect death will happen to me.*

Miranda recognized a dead end thought pattern and shuttered her mind. From long habit, she checked the adjoining bath and closet. A shower would be welcome, but it could wait. She pitched face down on the bed and was asleep in seconds.

CHAPTER 2

Garen LeRochefort gripped his satellite phone so hard the plastic dug into his hand. He'd been relieved when his operatives confirmed Miranda's plane was safe in New York City, but his relief was short-lived.

"Goddammit it all to hell." He snapped the phone shut.

People in the upscale lounge shot disapproving glances his way. Before Garen screamed that anyone who frequented a bar at six in the morning was nothing but a goddamned drunk, he beat a hasty retreat. He had no idea where Miranda was or even if she was still alive. He could call her, but her phone would likely be off. She was a good agent, and she followed protocols. One of the first was to keep communications gadgets not just off but also fully powered down since they could be used as tracking devices.

He laced his fingers together and squeezed until his hands ached. She'd been the obvious choice to send against Derek Roulan, head of the largest human trafficking ring on the globe. Roulan called his business International Success Ltd.—shortened to ISL—but the only one in the organization who succeeded was Roulan himself. Derek had an eye for ladies, and Miranda was one of the most exotic creatures Garen had ever laid eyes on. None of his male operatives would've stood a chance of getting close enough to Derek to handle him, and his other females weren't nearly as seductive.

Garen debated returning to his hotel room on the thirty-fifth floor. Instead, he opted for a walk. It was cold and sleeting in early morning Boston, but he needed something to quell the concern racing through him. Water ran down his face, but he ignored it. Pavement glistened in the light of a new day.

Garen was head of the U.S. branch of Rubicon International. Years before, he and Lars worked hard to come up with an apt name for their security firm, a euphemism to describe the dirty, wet work they engaged in. He'd actually thought it the joke of the century when much more modern spy operations adopted their company name. They'd been in business, under one guise or another, since just before the American Revolution.

Operating an undercover business had proven extremely useful to mask his long life—and come up with new documentation each time he faded out of one identity into another. Many of his employees were lycans like him, but some were other types of shifters. All of them were extremely long-lived. One of the modern day problems that had cropped up was that shifters were hunted— and imprisoned or killed if discovered. It meant he couldn't recruit outright. He and Lars operated a bit differently, but Garen had chosen to hire likely candidates and figure out along the way if they were shifters.

He'd tried to determine if Miranda fit the bill ever since she hired on, with no luck. At times, he'd been close, but she was wily, that one. She always slammed up a diversion to keep him out of her secret places. Damn, if he didn't want into those secret places—all of them. He imagined her long legs locked around his hips, and lust licked at him, hot and urgent.

He grimaced. Fantasizing about a naked Miranda was a nowhere street. Indulging himself with one of his employees would be just plain stupid. So why couldn't he get her out of his mind?

Garen did his damnedest to latch onto a shred of objectivity. He wouldn't do Miranda any good if he couldn't think straight. He sucked in a cold, soggy breath and followed it with another. It wasn't accidental he was in Boston. He'd wanted to be located on the East Coast in case something happened in Amsterdam, and he needed to catch a plane there. Hell, he would've staked out a presence in Europe, but he was too well-known. He didn't want his misplaced over-protectiveness to send up red flags that might end up killing his operative. Miranda could travel unnoticed. He couldn't.

He shook his head. After this assignment, assuming he got Miranda back in one piece, he'd have to rethink just how invisible she was. It was apparent Roulan's gang was after her. Deep inside, his wolf growled. It wanted to kill anything that might harm Miranda. He did what he could to calm it since shifting on the predawn streets of Boston was out of the question.

Lycans and other shifters were as close to *persona non grata* as criminals. If regular law enforcement got wind of them, they hunted them down and imprisoned or killed them. Garen exhaled sharply. The best part about Rubicon International was he had a trusted inner circle of operatives: fully vetted agents he trusted with his life.

In keeping with the total lack of trust shifters had in everyone, many—but certainly not all of them—showed up at a yearly gathering in their shifted form, never letting on who they were as humans. Sadness for his kind made his heart ache, but he shoved it aside. Emotions were an indulgence. He had more important places to focus his energy.

By the time he walked back through the fancy lobby of his hotel with its crystal chandeliers and plush furniture, he was wet enough other patrons gave him a wide berth. He sidled to the bank of elevators at the far side of the lobby. A lissome redhead followed him into one of the cars. Garen turned away. He knew what would come next.

"Hey there, handsome. A bit on the wet side, aren't we?"

"Drop it. I'm not interested."

She laughed, but it held a practiced edge. "You wouldn't need to worry about a thing, darling. Maybe just a nice massage and a hot bath—"

He glanced at the rapidly mounting numbers above the elevator door and pressed twenty-one since they weren't there yet. The door slid open. He grabbed the hooker's arm and pushed her into a carpeted hallway. "I said I'm not interested. Go ply your wares elsewhere."

He stabbed the *Close Door* button before she could leap back to his side with yet one more argument. Garen knew her kind. She was still attractive enough to be pushy and arrogant. He got out on the thirty-fifth floor, went to his room, and inserted his key card. His mouth twisted wryly. He wished a hooker could wipe Miranda out of his mind, but no one could. Everyone he'd fucked since he met her reminded him of her.

Garen stripped, dropping his wet clothes over a chair. "Yeah," he mumbled. "I want the one I can't have."

He started the water in the sunken tub and left the bathroom to check his phone. Nothing. He dialed Rubicon International's headquarters. It didn't take long to determine Miranda hadn't called in. His next call was to Lars' European branch of Rubicon, located in Heidelberg, Germany. All they could tell him—and they did it by inference—was that one of their other operatives was dead. Murdered at JFK, with his body stuffed into a parking lot dumpster.

Alarm fried Garen's nerve endings. His wolf became damn near uncontrollable. Claws shot from his toes. Before they could take over his hands, he turned the door's deadbolt and dropped the night-latch chain into its hasp. His body lengthened, fur sprouted, and he dropped to all fours. He loped around the generous suite until his tongue lolled. Garen loved the clean, unfettered animal energy. His wolf always knew what it wanted. Right now, it urged him to go after Miranda, but that wasn't practical since he had no idea where she was. Hopefully, she and Lars had gone to ground somewhere. As lethal an operative as himself, Lars was more than capable of taking care of business—assuming nothing had happened to him.

The sound of the tub filling changed. It took a moment before he understood water was pouring over the sides. In a flash, he reached for his human form and sprinted for the bathroom. He turned off the taps, pulled the plug, and sopped up the mess with a couple of thick towels. Once the water level had gone down a few inches, he levered himself into the tub and sat in the steaming water. It soothed his tight muscles but didn't relieve his worry.

He clenched a fist and banged it down on the side of the tub. *Damn it!* He needed a clear head, but all he could think about was Miranda—his Miranda—crouched behind a concrete wall defending herself. He should be by her side, helping her…

"No." He spoke out loud to get hold of his emotions. "She hasn't been through her final tests yet. Maybe once she's tenured, and I know beyond a shadow of doubt that she's a shifter, and I can trust her—"

Yeah, what then? Do I break every rule I ever made for Rubicon International and mate with her—make her mine?

Hold it right there, bud, a rational part of his brain horned in. She might not be lycan. It was remote, judging from her performance in the field, but still…

If she wasn't, he could always bite her and solve *that* little problem, but another of his rules would shatter. He'd forbidden lycans to create more of their kind until they were truly needed. No point in making shifters only to have them gunned down or carted off to a lifetime in a cell.

"Fuck."

A growl shook the bathroom. He got out of the tub and toweled himself off. "I made too many fucking rules, and now I'm falling over them." As an afterthought, he bent and pulled the plug, so the tub could drain.

∾

"I LET you sleep as long as I dared," Lars called from the doorway.

"Crap." Miranda rolled over and groaned. Her head pounded. Her body ached. Fear flooded her mouth with a sharp, metallic taste. "Why didn't I hear the door open?"

He grinned at her. "I can be quiet as a cat when I need to. I ordered breakfast. It should be here by the time you have had a shower." The door closed.

She lurched off the bed. The room spun, and she grabbed hold of a dresser until things steadied. Weak as a newborn pup, she shambled into the shower, dropping a trail of clothing as she went, and let hot jets pummel her body. Someone had outfitted the brownstone apartment since the shower was fully stocked, as was the rest of the bathroom.

Must be some kind of safe house, she surmised as she used lavender shampoo and soap. Her entire right side was one huge bruise from just below her breast all the way to her hipbone. More bruising trailed down the side of her leg. Miranda grimaced. Between being hurt and not remembering when she'd last eaten, no wonder she felt so shitty.

Lars stuck his head around the bathroom door she hadn't bothered to shut. "I put fresh clothes on the bed, *fraulein.*"

Miranda glanced at him through the glass shower doors and nodded. He could see her body, but it didn't matter. Or did it? Why wasn't he leaving? "Don't you have to take care of breakfast or something?" she called over the noise of the shower.

He laughed wryly. "It is here. Your side looks...serious. Would you like me to wrap it?"

"Do you have an Ace wrap that big?"

"Of course. My firm maintains this apartment."

She pressed her tongue against her teeth. "Just leave the bandage on the bed. I'll manage."

"It is better if I do it, *fraulein.* You will not get it tight enough."

"I'll think about it. Now get out of here, so I can finish up."

"Your wish is my command."

Miranda snorted back laughter. Once he was gone, she shut off the water, swathed her long, wet hair in one towel, and used another to dry herself. A cursory examination of the medicine cabinet yielded toothpaste and half a dozen toothbrushes wrapped in plastic. She brushed her teeth. Between soap, water, and moving around, she felt a little better.

A nondescript pair of black pants along with an oversized black shirt and black jacket lay on the bed. Clean underwear—panties and a jog bra—had been placed atop them, along with an enormous Ace wrap. Miranda held the pile of clothing to her nose and breathed deep.

Clean. What a luxury. She slid into the underwear and tried wrapping the elasticized bandage around her ribs. Lars had been right. The angle was awkward.

She blew out a breath and made a decision. Pants, bra, and boots on, she put the top and jacket over one arm, grabbed the bandage, and opened her bedroom door. The smells of breakfast hit her in the face.

Famished. I'm famished.

She raced into the front room ready to inhale whatever had arrived for breakfast.

Lars got to his feet as soon as he saw her. He pried the Ace wrap out of her hands. "Stand still. Put your arms out to your sides."

"Can't we do this after I eat?" Saliva filled her mouth. She swallowed, or it would've run down her chin.

"This will only take a minute. It is best when your muscles are warm from the shower." Expert fingers wove the bandage around her and fastened it with metal butterfly clips. "There, *fraulein*. Now you may eat."

Miranda was in such a hurry to get to the food, she nearly forgot to drag the black stretchy top over her head. She plowed through toast slathered with butter and jam, bacon, ham, and eggs, not bothering with conversation. Lars kept her coffee cup filled and remained quiet. He seemed hungry too, though he'd obviously eaten while she cleaned up. Once her blood sugar was heading in the right direction—back up—she took a deep breath.

"Better. I feel lots better." She eyed him. "Do you know anything?"

He nodded but didn't elaborate.

Her temper, always a liability, sparked. "Well—" she slammed a fist on the table "—if you know something, goddammit, tell me."

The corners of his mouth twitched. "Garen is in Boston. We will meet him in—" he glanced at his phone "—about five hours at one of the smaller airports just outside town."

Her mouth fell open; her heart sped up. "Garen?" She shook her head. "You must be mistaken. He's in Seattle. Why would he be here?" Miranda narrowed her eyes. "It's a trap. Part of what happened last night. The bastards who are after me haven't given up—"

"Stop." His cold, gray gaze augured into her. "Give me a little credit, *fraulein*." He cocked his head to one side. "My guess is he was worried about your assignment and moved closer to the East Coast in case he had to...do something."

She slugged back more coffee. "It sounds as if you know him. Do you?"

He shrugged noncommittally. "Of course. In this business, we all know one another."

"I didn't mean like that." She hesitated. "We don't *all know one another*. After all, I just met you at the Amsterdam airport. It sounds like you're well enough acquainted with Garen to second-guess his motives."

Lars didn't answer.

Miranda polished off the rest of the food on her plate and opened the foam boxes to make certain she hadn't missed anything. She glanced at Lars. "How are we going to get from here to Boston?"

"We will drive. There should be a car waiting out front."

She thought about the geography of the East Coast. "Shouldn't we be leaving?"

He nodded. *"Ja.* Grab your things."

She glanced at their mess. "Do you want me to straighten up?"

He brayed laughter. *"Fraulein.* Most agents are men. We are not good housekeepers. Someone will be along to take care of things."

~

Lars drove the silver Lexus RX 450 with the same easy assurance he'd flown the Gulfstream. At his insistence, she covered her hair with a black baseball cap and slumped low in the plush leather passenger seat. She tried to engage him in conversation. Instead, he turned the satellite radio to a channel that played German opera. Wagner's *Tristan und Isolde* blared from the speakers.

Everything she'd eaten sat in her stomach like a brick until they cleared the outskirts of New York City. Once it appeared their car wasn't on the bad guys' wanted list, she relaxed enough to digest her meal. Miranda's thoughts turned inward. It was actually a relief that Lars wasn't hitting on her like he'd done last night. Not that he wasn't attractive…

She glanced sidelong at him through slitted eyes and nodded to herself. She'd sell her soul if he wasn't a shifter. What was that he'd said about being quiet as a cat? She opened her mouth to ask but then shut it. No point in making him believe she was interested. Or in bringing up shifters—a forbidden topic in polite company.

Like it usually did when she let it drift, her mind turned to Garen.

Miranda felt a funny flutter behind her breastbone. In just a little while, she'd see him in the flesh. The prospect took her breath away. She barely spent any time with him back at Rubicon International's offices. He was usually on the top floor where his office was, and she was down in the bullpen with other agents who'd not yet been tenured.

She dragged her cell phone out of her bag. Her finger hovered over the power button.

"Do not do that."

Her head snapped up. She'd nearly forgotten about Lars. "Not safe yet?"

"*Fraulein*. After what I believe you did, you will not be *safe* anywhere for a very long time."

A chill ran down her back. "Okay. So I'll get a new phone."

"At the very least. You might want to consider plastic surgery. No way to disguise your height, but a competent surgeon could—"

"No!" The vehemence in her voice surprised her, but her wolf was in full rebellion. "No fucking way. I'll consider colored contact lenses and maybe bleaching my hair, but that's the end of it."

He shrugged, a rather Gaelic gesture given his Teutonic bloodlines. "It is your funeral."

"Are you trying to scare me?" Miranda kept her voice steady.

"Maybe. I believe in being practical. Your target concerned Garen enough, he traveled thousands of miles to be nearby if he was needed. Do not underestimate the danger." An oblique glance from Lars' gray eyes grazed her, sharp as shrapnel.

"Fine. So I'm fucked." She crossed her arms over her chest. The motion made her ribs ache. "At least the bad guy's dead."

Savage laughter filled the car. "Good for you, *fraulein*. You have spirit. Hang onto it. How did you end up an operative?"

The question came out of left field. She launched into an answer before she realized what she was doing. "I was a Green Beret stationed in the Middle East. I had some, er, issues with Army policies." She bit her lower lip, wondering how much to tell him.

"I would rather you did not feed me a carefully constructed lie, *fraulein*. One of two things happened. Either they kicked you out for insubordination—"

"Stop." She held up a hand and gathered shards of dignity about herself. "When my term ended, I chose not to reenlist."

"Why?"

"None of your business."

He snorted. "You guessed correctly last night. I have been in a few branches of the military." He cleared his throat. "For those of us who appreciate latitude in how we fulfill our assignments, it can be a bit confining."

She snorted right back. "No shit." Miranda sucked in a breath. She'd just shared more information with Lars than she'd shared with anyone in the years she'd worked for Rubicon International. Agents didn't discuss anything personal with one another. It was as if they hadn't had lives before becoming Rubicon employees. And agents like her—not-yet-vetted ones—knew less than nothing. All information was on a *need to know* basis.

She sucked in a breath, wincing as her ribcage expanded. "I told you some things. You tell me how you know Garen."

For a moment, she thought he was going to shut her down, but then he started talking.

*G*aren pulled his fur-lined leather jacket closer to his body. He paced up and down the asphalt in front of the private airport just north of Boston and glanced at his phone again.

Damn it. They should have been here half an hour ago.

What the fuck had happened? He shook his head and paced some more, grinding his teeth together until his jaws ached.

Their plane sat on the tarmac, waiting. Garen had spent a few moments admiring the sleek Learjet Challenger 300. He was looking forward to copiloting it. If he wasn't so anxious, he might've grinned. He and Lars had flown *sub rosa* missions in and out of nearly every shithole on earth. They made a hell of a team—and had for hundreds of years.

His phone vibrated in his pocket. Garen made a grab for it and looked at the display. It said *Private*. Not a bad thing, all in all. Everyone in his business put permanent blocks on their caller ID. He punched the talk key and waited. No reason for him to say anything until he knew who'd called.

"We are close. Problems with traffic and road closures." Lars' deep voice was welcome.

A breath he didn't know he'd been holding whooshed out of Garen, and he loosened his grip on the phone. "ETA?" he barked.

"Maybe two minutes." Lars chuckled. "Although I must admit I would prefer my time with the fair *fraulein* was not drawing to a close."

What?

Garen practically choked on, "Really?" He was surprised just how neutral his tone sounded. "And why would that be?" Stomach muscles tense, he waited for an answer that might destroy him. Had Lars taken up with Miranda? It was possible. Lars told him they'd spent the night together in one of Rubicon's many safe house. A vision of Miranda's black hair mingling with Lars' blond locks made Garen nauseous.

"She is warming to me. I just know it. See you very soon, old friend."

Call Ended flared across the display.

Garen stared at his phone and clenched his jaws. He had to get control of himself before they showed up, or he might rip Lars' head off.

Tires crunched on gravel. Garen turned toward the sound and saw a silver SUV heading toward him. Long years of caution took over. He strolled to the terminal, pushed the glass door open, and stood off to one side. Because it catered to military personnel flying incognito, this airport was outfitted with bulletproof glass.

Lars' unmistakable profile came into view. The figure slouched in the passenger seat had to be Miranda. Garen's wolf was beside himself, yapping and whining. The wolf wanted Miranda, had wanted her ever since she'd come to work for Rubicon International. He thought she was a shifter, but the wolf's assessment of such things had been wrong more than once.

Garen shoved his animal side deep, pasted a small smile—not too exuberant—on his face, and went to meet them. Lars leapt out first. Garen extended a hand, but the other man swept him into a hug and kissed both cheeks. "It has been a long road. I am glad to see you." Familiar gray eyes crinkled at the corners.

Garen nodded to himself. He and Lars went back a long way. If his oldest friend had taken up with Miranda, he'd suck it up and wish them every happiness. It would damn near kill him, but he'd figure it out. The other car door opened. He extricated himself from Lars and went to greet his employee. His eyes widened. "Holy shit, Miran— er, Jayne. You look like hell."

A corner of her mouth turned down. "Thanks, boss. I think." She twisted around to drag her carry-on out of the SUV and groaned.

"Are you injured?"

Lars walked up to them. "She has deep contusions. I taped her torso. It is all a doctor would have done."

Years of undercover work took over. So Lars had not only seen Miranda unclothed, he'd even bandaged her. Garen wiped his face clean of expression and tipped his chin up. "Are you certain she's fit to travel?"

"I'm right here." Miranda sounded irritated. "Of course I can travel. I just sat in a car for four plus hours." She moved right in front of Garen, so he had to look at her. "If you want to know how I am, ask me."

"Yes, ma'am." He inclined his head and hoped to hell his emotions—jealousy, pride, and a touch of amusement—weren't visible on his face.

"You grow them feisty these days," Lars noted wryly. "Do you have luggage?"

"It's already in the plane. I took the liberty of filing our flight plan."

Lars grinned. "Excellent. One less thing to do." He grabbed his bag out of the car and made a sweeping motion with one arm. "After you."

Garen's forehead creased. "What about the car?"

"My instructions were to leave the keys in it. Someone will come round to pick it up." Lars hooked an arm through Miranda's.

Garen bit down so hard he thought his teeth might crack. "Not what I meant. This isn't Europe. You can't just leave the car parked in the middle of the street."

"But it is not—"

"Either you move it, or I will." Garen crossed his arms across his chest.

Lars rolled his eyes. "You are in a true snit, my friend. Once we are airborne, you must tell me what is wrong." He ducked gracefully into the Lexus and manipulated it into a parking spot a few yards away.

Like hell I will. What would I say? Miranda doesn't belong to me.

He glanced sideways at Miranda. She stared back. "Coming?" he inquired gruffly. "I can take your bag."

"I'll take it myself," she snapped. "Is that our plane?" She pointed. At his nod, she turned abruptly and headed for it.

Feeling like a fool, he clumped after her. What he wanted to do was grill her, make her tell him exactly what had happened between her and Lars, but it would be a mistake. For one thing, it wasn't any of his affair—not really. For another, she could fuck whoever she chose. He had no right to dictate her choices.

I don't have any idea what transpired...

He tried to soothe himself as he caught up to Miranda. And then he remembered how Lars had taken her arm with a proprietary air. He set his wolf to sniffing, but all it smelled was soap and shampoo. She'd showered this morning and washed off the evidence.

Miranda stopped at the foot of the stairs leading into the Learjet and spun to face him. "Why are you angry with me? I fulfilled my assignment." Her mouth was set in a hard line. "I'll admit it wasn't the cleanest job I've ever pulled off, but I'm lucky I'm still alive. Getting next to Roulan was like waltzing into a serpent's den and pretending they couldn't see me. I was so scared, I was almost paralyzed."

Lars trotted up. Garen balled his hands into fists. He needed to talk with Miranda. Had to find out what had happened in Amsterdam. He knew Roulan was dead, but lacked details.

Almost as if Lars could read his thoughts, he murmured, "Let us get aboard. I will have my headset on. You can turn yours off for privacy, so she can report in."

Garen felt like an ass. Lars truly was his oldest friend. A mountain cat in his other form, the man was a formidable ally and the other half of Rubicon International's sprawling spy empire. Garen would be a fool to do anything to erode their long partnership. He felt his cheeks heat. Lars quirked an inquisitive brow but didn't say anything before mounting the stairs and entering the plane.

Miranda followed him. Garen came last and secured the door. "I'm going to sit in the copilot's seat until we're airborne," he told her. "We can talk after the plane hits cruise altitude."

"Gee." Her tone was acidic. "I can hardly wait."

Garen winced. He actually deserved that. "Look." He made a huge effort and kept his hands to himself rather than laying one on her shoulder. "I'm sorry. If I'm snarky, it's because I was worried half sick about you."

She drew back as if he'd bitten her. "Don't go getting all maudlin on me, boss. It's a job, remember? I've seen lots of people die. So have you. Emotions cut into our concentration. I've heard you preach to the group often enough. Cold, clear detachment—"

The whine of a jet turbine interrupted her words. "Hang onto that thought, Miranda," he half shouted. "I'll be back soon." Garen strode toward the cockpit. She was right. Embarrassment made his stomach clench. This wasn't the time to drag her into his arms and tell her he'd been watching her for years, had waited for her for nearly that long…

"I need you to sit so we can take off." Lars held out a headset. Beyond his accent, his voice was devoid of inflection.

Garen dropped into the right seat, buckled in, and settled the headphones in place. Static crackled when Lars communicated with the tower. He nosed the plane into line. "We are third to depart."

"Yes, I heard that too."

"What is wrong? You do not seem like yourself."

Garen shook his head. "Don't mind me. I didn't get much sleep last night."

Lars drew the throttle back to idle when he came nose to tail with the jet ahead of them in line for takeoff. He turned and looked at Garen, his features elegant with feline grace. "You had nothing to fear, my friend. Miranda was with me. I have not lost an operative yet."

Garen couldn't help it. He laughed. Lars was the same arrogant shifter he'd always been. "No, my friend." He mimicked Lars' accent. "We've sacrificed a hell of a lot of civilians keeping our operatives safe, though."

"Don't remind me." Lars scowled and turned his attention back to the Plexiglas windscreen. "She is exquisite. I can see why you would be so concerned about keeping her safe. Barely leashed power bleeds off her. What is she?"

Garen dropped his gaze. "She's close to her final test. Until then, I'm often not positive about any of my agents."

A long, low whistle filled the cockpit. "Yes. I recall that. It is one place where Rubicon's policies differ. We find out much sooner at our Heidelberg center. No point in investing all that training if we end up jettisoning an agent for lack of magical ability."

"It isn't that I haven't tried," Garen protested. "Every time I get close, she slithers away."

Lars made a clicking sound. "*Tch.* Maybe you did not have quite the right touch." Before Garen could inquire acidly just what Lars thought the *right touch* might be, the other man said, "Here we go." He gave the powerful engines a healthy dose of jet fuel. They roared merrily and sent them barreling down the runway and into the sky.

❧

MIRANDA TWISTED IN HER SEAT. It was hard to get comfortable. She thought about unwrapping the bandage but was afraid it might make things worse. She'd actually been feeling pretty chipper until they met up with Garen. It was obvious he was unhappy with her. Problem was, she couldn't figure out why. Not that he'd ever paid much attention to her beyond giving her orders, but at least he'd been pleasant on those occasions.

She teased out scents. Anger, jealousy, fear, possession. Anger was the only one that made sense. She had no idea how many agents worked for Rubicon International, but there were lots—maybe hundreds if you considered their many offices scattered around the globe. She'd find out more about RI once she passed her final set of tests and because a fully vetted agent. Why Garen would be so spun out over one junior-grade operative didn't make a lick of sense.

Footsteps sounded, and he settled in the seat across from her. She studied his face, but his expression didn't yield a single clue. He removed his headset, clicked it off, and then inclined his head and met her gaze.

Miranda gathered her thoughts while she removed her own headset and turned it to the off position. She nodded crisply. "Sir."

Something must've clicked because he said, "Report."

Aha! Commands were a comfort zone—for both of them.

"Brief, full, or extensive, sir?"

"Somewhere between full and extensive. Tell me what I need to know."

She sucked in a breath. "I arrived in Amsterdam without incident and went to my hotel. From there, I scoped out the strip club our target frequents. I inquired whether they needed another dancer." Miranda twisted her mouth into a sour expression. "The sicko who ran the place wanted his own private show, so I gave it to him."

Garen furled his brows. "And?"

She half snorted a laugh. "Bastard came the second I wrapped my hand around him. But he did hire me. I returned to the hotel, got some food, slept a couple of hours, and went back to the club. I was into my third set with half a dozen other girls. It was getting late, maybe three a.m., and I was worried Roulan wasn't going to show."

She exhaled noisily. The next part was when things had gone to hell.

Garen gestured for her to continue.

She nodded, her thoughts racing as she remembered. The overweight Romanian with greasy, black hair and little piggy eyes was disgusting. He stank of sweat and rancid food. He'd come into the club with four other men and a group of girls who looked young, barely into puberty. The group had settled at a ringside table.

Miranda nervously pushed hair over her shoulders and sat straighter. "Roulan finally showed up, noticed me right away, and beckoned me over. Made me lap dance for him and the man sitting next to him. It was quite delicate. I had to keep their hands busy everywhere but between my legs where I had a small gun strapped to my thigh."

She swallowed, but her mouth was dry. She could still feel his nasty fingers pinching her breasts and bottom. "The Fasten Seatbelt sign is still on. Do you suppose I could get myself some water?"

Something flickered behind Garen's eyes. It might've been kindness, but he hooded them before she could be certain. "Lars probably forgot to turn it off. I'll get you a bottle. We're at cruise altitude."

He rustled in the galley across from the head and returned with cheese, crackers, bottled water, and a microbrewed beer. He raised an eyebrow. "Beer might sit well."

She favored him with a wan smile and reached for the water. "Maybe once I'm done talking." A flick of her wrist and she removed the cap and drank. Water dribbled down her chin. She wiped it with the back of her hand. "Better. It's probably not important, but Roulan had six young girls with him. If any of them were over thirteen, I'd be shocked. They were made up like whores." She shut her eyes for a moment. "The whole thing made me sick."

"It also makes it easier to do the work we do." His voice was soft.

She twitched her lip into a sneer. "No kidding. I wanted to wring his neck long before I ended up alone with him, but I'm getting ahead of myself." She took another drink. "He more or less ordered me to come upstairs with him and his buddies." At the shocked look that blossomed on Garen's face, she shook her head. "Pah. I know better. I told him I'd dance for him, but just for him. In the meantime, I'd been trying to maneuver so I could drop a poison capsule I had tucked in my bra into his drink, but his men watched me like hawks. It wasn't dark enough to do the sleight of hand I needed to pull off something like that."

Miranda drained the water bottle and forged ahead. The sooner she got done with this story, the better she'd like it. "Roulan jumped up and grabbed me around the waist." She tried to maintain a professional demeanor but wasn't able to suppress a shudder. "Ugh. He smelled so bad, it was all I could do not to knee him in the balls and judo chop him right there in front of everyone. His teeth were rotting and... It doesn't matter. I followed him upstairs. Two of his men trailed after us. I stopped at the top of the stairs and told him I wasn't interested in servicing his men."

Garen couldn't hide the concern etching his forehead into deep lines. "Cut to the chase, Miranda."

"He reassured me it would only be us and that his men were there to guard the door. He obviously knew his way around the upper level of the club because he seized my wrist and nearly dragged me into a room that was tricked out like a cheap bordello. Once we were inside, he laid himself on the bed, unzipped his trousers, and dragged his cock out. He told me to take my clothes off, so I guess he planned to work on himself while I stripped."

Miranda fisted her hands in her lap and forced herself to take a deep breath. "I knew that wouldn't work. I had to be closer to him, so I took off my top and slipped out of my gauzy pants. For once, my thigh holster and gun slid down without a hitch. He was so busy jacking himself, I'm sure he didn't notice me bury them in my clothes. Anyway, I waltzed over to him and asked him to suck on my breasts. The second he lowered his head, I buried my hands in his greasy hair, got him in the cranial nerves, and rendered him unconscious."

"Sounds pretty clean so far."

"Yeah, that's what I thought. I was getting ready to kill him, but even though I hadn't made any noise, somehow his men knew—" She hesitated. "I'm not certain they knew he was out, but they knew something was wrong. I heard a commotion outside the door and made a dive for my gun. They raced into the room. I shot one. That's when Roulan somehow regained his senses. Next thing I knew, he was hammering me in the side with a lead pipe."

"Christ." A disgusted look curled Garen's finely modeled mouth into a scowl.

Shame filled her, and her cheeks grew warm. "I'm sorry, boss. I know I botched it. But how was I to know Roulan's men had some sort of paranormal link to him?"

"Keep talking. Two against one aren't bad odds." He shot an appraising glance her way. If there'd been concern on his face earlier, it had fled. "What happened then?"

I turned into a wolf and killed both of them while their mouths were still hanging open... Crap! I can't tell him that.

"Um, I got lucky. Wrenched the lead pipe away from Roulan and brained him with it. The other guy tried to run. Caught him in the back of the head with the pipe before he made the stairway."

Garen eyed her intently. She looked away, studying her hands. There was no way he could tell she'd just lied to him. Or was there?

To cover her discomfiture, Miranda hurried on. "I knew I didn't have much time before everyone in the place converged on the upstairs room. I bundled my clothes, tied them around my waist, and went out a window. Lucky for me those old buildings are made of uneven stonework. I've never climbed down anything so fast.

Once I hit the street, I disappeared into an alley so I could throw my costume on. After that, I ran like hell, flagged a cab, and headed for my hotel so I could get my bag and my clothes."

"You should've gone straight to the airport."

"Really? My breasts were hanging out of a barely-there top. I was wearing harem pants and sandals in cold weather. And carrying a snub-nosed .38."

"Mmph." He cleared his throat. "I stand corrected. Still, you're fortunate you weren't followed to your hotel."

"No one knew where I was staying. The creep who owned the nightclub never asked for my passport or any kind of ID. Even if he had, I'd have given him one of the phony ones other than Jayne Powers."

"Still. They got a good look at you. You'll have to go to ground for a while."

She bit her lip. She'd been afraid of that. "I'd really rather not, sir. I like being busy. Not sure what I'd do with myself."

"Not your choice, Miss Miller."

Crap! He never calls me by my last name.

Miranda wanted to bury her head in her hands. Instead, she met his bright-blue gaze. "I'd like to turn this into a learning experience, sir. Please tell me what I did wrong."

An odd look flitted across his face. "You can discuss that with the other junior agents once you return." He pushed to his feet. "I'll be in the cockpit if you need me." He picked up the unopened beer and pushed it into her lap. "You're looking a little pale, Miss Miller. Drink up. It will be several hours before we land."

CHAPTER 4

Garen hesitated fractionally before opening the cockpit door. If there'd been anywhere else in the plane to go, he would've headed for it. He needed to be alone, so he could process what Miranda had told him. She'd lied about how she dispatched Roulan and his man, but why? What did she have to hide?

It's the same fucking reason she keeps me out of her mind.

Anger flared so hot it shocked him. He raised a fist to pound on the molded partition next to the cockpit door but stopped himself. For a moment, he wondered if she weren't some sort of double agent who'd infiltrated Rubicon International. He shook his head and let himself into the cockpit.

Lars glanced at him. "Excellent. I'd like to take a break and stretch my legs. Your airplane."

Garen settled into the right seat. "Got it," he snapped through clenched teeth.

Lars drew his blond brows together. He looked on the edge of saying something. Instead, he turned and left the cockpit. Jealousy added fuel to the fire raging in Garen's breast. He wondered if Lars would take advantage of Miranda's obviously distraught state to comfort her, and nearly drove himself mad. Finally, he tuned in his wolf senses and tried to listen for conversation in the cabin. He didn't have to wait long.

"You are looking distraught, *fraulein*. Are you all right?"

"No." Miranda's voice held a bitten-off quality. Garen smiled to himself. It sounded as if she'd just told Lars to piss up a rope.

"Do not fear. I will see you safely home once we land."

Garen tensed his hand on the yoke and strained to make certain he heard her response.

"That's kind of you. I may not be very good company, but I accept. It beats spending fifty bucks on a cab."

"Then it is settled, *fraulein*. You are still not recovered. Try to close your beautiful eyes."

Garen filled his lungs with little, panting gasps of air. His wolf was nearly uncontrollable. Not that Lars hadn't seen his animal form, but still it had no place in the Learjet's cockpit. A feral possessiveness roiled through him, so intense he thought he might vomit. Where was Lars? Had he sat down next to Miranda to draw her into his arms?

Pay attention to the aircraft, an inner voice hissed.

Why? It's on autopilot.

In case the sensors miss something, you asshole.

"Great," he mumbled. "Now I'm talking with myself."

"You always did, old friend."

Garen turned abruptly. He'd been so lost in misery he didn't heard the snick of the latch when Lars let himself back into the cockpit. The other man settled into the left seat and plugged his headset into the instrument cluster. He glanced at Garen and said, "My airplane," to spell out who was controlling the aircraft.

"All yours." Garen tried to infuse neutrality into the statement.

Apparently it didn't work because Lars asked, "Would you like to talk about what is eating at you?"

"Not particularly."

"Humph. Did she tell you what happened in Amsterdam?"

"Not all of it."

A knowing look swept over Lars' features. "Did she leave things out or lie?"

Garen shook his head. "I'm not certain if she left anything out, but she lied about how two of the men died."

Lars' nostrils twitched. "I tell you, she is like us—some sort of shifter. If I were a betting man, I would believe she changed to whatever animal she is and dispatched them in that fashion."

"You'd think she'd trust me after all these years," Garen groused.

Lars shrugged. "Why? Humans who can take animal forms are hunted and killed. Why would she trust anyone with information like that—if she wished to live?" He paused. "I understand how sensitive you are to anything that smacks of criticism, but I told you years ago to weed agents out long before you do. Figure out who the shifters are within the first year or so. It would save you much time and unhappiness."

Defensiveness heated Garen's face. "How I run Rubicon International on my side of the Atlantic has worked well enough. There's no reliable way to recruit for shifters, so I've chosen to sort through which agents will work for us the old fashioned way. Through observation and training. The second I know someone isn't one of us, I jettison them."

Another shrug. "*Ja*, but you have lost a few shifters too, as I recall. Agents who could have been salvaged had they felt comfortable enough trusting you with their secrets. They became disillusioned long before their final set of tests and left our employ."

Garen grunted. Lars made a good point, but Garen was damned if he'd admit it. "I've always been afraid someone would infiltrate the operation. It's why I've kept the fully vetted ones—agents I'd trust with my life—separate from the others."

"Just because you have always done things a certain way is not a reason to maintain something, if it no longer serves you." Lars hesitated. "The computer era has made it much more difficult for our kind to hide what we are. Our walls have grown thicker, more impenetrable, out of necessity. Had you created a more open environment, invited your agents-in-training to—"

"Your point?" Garen broke in acidly.

Yet a third shrug. "I am not certain I have a point, my friend. We are merely making conversation."

Like hell we are.

It was on the tip of his tongue to ask about Lars' intentions toward Miranda, but he didn't. Garen uncurled his fingers from the yoke. Parachuting out of the plane seemed like a great option—except they were cruising at thirty-five thousand feet.

"Sorry not to give this a rest, but if you are not willing to talk with me, probably your oldest friend, then whom?"

Garen shook his head. He didn't have an answer. He'd known Miranda was off limits when he started lusting after her years before. It was too late now. The die was cast. No way he could go backward and command his brain—and his dick, never mind his wolf—to stop yearning for her. "Thanks for the offer," he muttered. "I'll think about it."

A corner of Lars' mouth twitched. "While you are thinking, how are we going to keep her safe?"

Garen didn't have to ask who the *her* was. "She'll need to rent a hotel room for a while, at least until I can position agents around her apartment. We'll find out soon enough who's after her. Although, it would practically have to be ISL." He sucked in a tense breath. "Miranda's stubborn. She's not going to like this development."

"It is for her own good."

Garen snorted and bit back a wry laugh. "You know that. So do I. The problem will be getting her to see it. Damned woman thinks she's invincible."

"I rest my case. She has to be one of us." Lars grinned. "Shifters are the only ones with quite that brand of arrogance. I offered to take her home once we land. Leave it to me to convince her to stay in a hotel. I will make certain to book us, er, her into a very upscale lodging."

Garen clacked his teeth together with a sharp snap. "I'd rather you didn't."

Lars furled his brows. "Why not?" Understanding flooded his sharp-boned face. Pale stubble stood out along his jawline. "I see. You wish her for yourself."

"I am not going to discuss this."

Lars ignored him. "Does she return your affections?"

Garen stared out the windscreen. He felt Lars' gaze move over him. Damn it, anyway. The man didn't miss squat. He opened his mouth, but Lars waved him to silence. "You need not say a word. I can read the whole, sad tale on your face."

Garen grabbed Lars' arm across the few feet separating their seats. "You will not say a word to her. Do I make myself clear?"

"Abundantly." Lars' nostrils flared. "I had not planned to. It will make it easier to—"

"Don't say it." Garen's tongue felt glued to the roof of his mouth.

"All right. Just remember, old friend, you have had years to declare yourself. If she decides I am the better choice, who could blame her?"

Garen slammed out of the cockpit. It was either that or drive a fist through Lars' grinning face.

Miranda's eyes flew open when the cockpit door crashed against the wall. Garen looked ready to kill something. He swept by her and went into the head.

Holy Christ! Wonder what went wrong between him and Lars?

She rubbed the bridge of her nose between her thumb and index fingers and stared out the window. They'd been chasing dusk across the country. It was still light enough to see mountains below.

Must be the Rockies. Great. Means we're not too far from home.

She sat up in her seat and rotated first one shoulder and then the other. God, but her ribs ached. She supposed the bruising had continued to spread. It did that until all the subterranean blood vessels sealed themselves. Maybe going to ground for a while wasn't all that bad an idea. She could spend time in her wolf form, which would speed the healing process. It would also put some distance between herself and the disapproval in Garen's blue eyes.

An unpleasant thought clawed its way forward. Maybe she didn't have a future with Rubicon International. They fired agents for botched jobs; she'd seen it happen indirectly. Agents—the unvetted ones—disappeared, never to be seen again. Her heart ached for far more than the possible loss of her job. If Garen fired her, she'd never see him again.

Don't be a fool, she told herself. *He scarcely even knows I'm alive— except for right now when he sees me as a gross inconvenience.*

For the barest moment, she imagined his blue eyes alight with lust, his body skin to skin against hers, his lips hard and demanding as they trailed down her body and settled on a nipple, sucking and teasing… She pressed her thighs together to quell the ache in her nether regions. She'd take care of herself once Garen left the head. Miranda forced her mind away from her swollen clit.

Sex is a waste of time. What I need are employment alternatives.

She narrowed her eyes as she considered her options. She'd left the Army in good standing. They'd probably take her back in a heartbeat. Fully trained field agents didn't grow on trees. An inner voice reminded her that she hadn't reenlisted because she hated the regimentation, but she shushed it.

Her wolf howled in protest. The armed forces weren't conducive to that side of her ever coming out to romp. She'd even had to give up the annual gathering—the one time each year when shifters shucked their human form and met in secret to just be animals and play. The Army kept close tabs on their Green Beret force. She'd never trusted them not to tail her, even when she wasn't on duty.

Her mind drifted to Lucifer, head of the lycans. A powerful

leader, he was also the most gorgeous wolf she'd ever seen, with his black and silver pelt and silvery eyes. He'd stepped in and organized them, ruling via a combination of telepathy and scrambled electronic transmissions. Things had improved for lycans since he'd scrapped his way to the top of the heap. And for other shifters as well. Of course, there were things he had no control over, but at least they'd gotten better at hiding their dual natures. His prohibition against biting helped too, since it kept their numbers manageable. As he'd pointed out, they could always create new lycans. The trick was maintaining a dynamic balance, so they remained off everyone's radar.

"If those in power forget our existence," he'd growled at the last gathering, "we can breathe a bit."

Miranda always hoped she'd be one of the females he picked to couple with at the gathering. So far, though, she hadn't been able to talk herself into getting close enough to even try.

Story of my life. Both of them actually—wolf and human. The guy I want never wants me...

"Penny for your thoughts, Miss Miller?"

Miranda nearly jumped out of her seat. She ran up against her lap belt and fell against the thickly padded leather of her contoured chair. "How did you manage to sneak up on me like that?"

He eyed her. "I can be quiet when I want to be."

"Yes, but I didn't even hear the john door open." She blew out a breath. "I'm usually more on top of things."

"You've had a rough go of it." He took the seat across from hers that he'd sat in earlier and reached over to tap her empty beer bottle. "Would you like another?"

"How much longer until we land?"

He pulled his phone from a pocket and glanced at the time. "A little over an hour. I'm thinking we'd be better served to land in Olympia or Bellingham. We can rent a car and drive the rest of the way." He keyed his headset and asked Lars which airport he preferred.

Miranda turned on her headset but missed Lars' answer. She glanced at Garen. "You think ISL will have Sea-Tac staked out."

"It's what I'd do if I were them."

"What'd Lars say about airports?"

"He voted for Bellingham. I tend to agree with him. It's smaller and more out of the way."

They're doing this to protect me.

She tossed half a smile at Garen. "Thanks."

He cocked his head to one side. "Not angry anymore?"

"I've had a few hours to think. I agree I need to drop out of sight at least for a couple of weeks."

"Thank Christ you've come to your senses. I was afraid I'd have to knock you out and lock you in a safe house with twenty-four-hour guards."

He blew out an audible breath, and she understood how worried he was. In their business, people didn't talk about things like that. Worry and fear could deep-six any operation. Negative emotions tended to feed on themselves, so agents shoved them in a psychic cellar and barred the door with chains.

"Do you have a safe house where I can stay?"

He nodded. "Either that or a hotel. Your choice."

"Are any of the safe houses outside the city?"

He frowned. "Why?"

She ginned up what she hoped was a noncommittal expression. "No particular reason. It just seemed safer to be outside the I-5 corridor."

"You'd be more isolated if something were to go wrong."

"Cuts both ways. They'll have a harder time finding me if I remain out of sight. Besides, I think Lars will stay with me at least for a while."

Something flashed across Garen's face, but it was gone so fast she couldn't identify it. He made a sound between a snort and a snarl.

"Really? When did the two of you get to be such close friends?"

Heat rushed upward from her chest to her face. "We're not. He's just a nice man who offered to help me. I don't understand why that bothers you. I'm guessing you hired him for this operation just like you hired me. Besides, from what he told me, the two of you go back a long way."

This time she read Garen easily. Surprise etched his features.

"What did he tell you?"

"About how the two of you used to fly fugitives in and out of some hot spots."

He crooked two fingers her way. "What else?"

Her already warm face got even hotter. She was certain every freckle was visible. "Uh, just a little about the women you shared on some of your missions."

Garen's eyes widened. "He told you about that. Shit! What was he thinking?"

To hell with Lars' motives. I'm not discussing sex with the man I've been fantasizing about fucking for years.

"Don't give it another thought, boss. Things like that are really common in life-and-death situations." She waved a dismissive hand, desperate to change the subject.

"Oh, and how would you know?"

Something feral blazed behind his eyes. Her wolf smelled his arousal and wanted to jump him. Here. Now. She shoved her animal side deeper. Men. All you had to do was mention sex, and they were off and running.

Yeah, well, I'm not far behind.

She straightened in her seat, realized she'd just shoved her breasts toward him, and forced her body to relax against the cushy chair. Her clit throbbed. Her nipples formed hard points that had to be visible through the fabric of her top. "Maybe because I've been there a time or two. It's not like I'm a child. I'm nearly thirty. Can we go back to talking about where I'll be staying?"

"Why?" He ran his tongue over his lips and leaned toward her.

"I'm rather enjoying this conversational thread, Miss Miller." A delectable, spice-saturated, musky scent rolled off him in waves.

She couldn't help herself. She squirmed against her seat. Actually squirmed. The pressure of her thighs rubbing together nearly made her come. Her breath came fast enough he had to notice. She stole a glance at his lap, and then wished she hadn't. The swell of his erection tented his pants. It took all her self-control not to make a dive for his zipper.

CHAPTER 5

Garen threw caution to the four winds. He clicked off his headset and tossed it into the next seat. His cock pressed mercilessly against the front of his pants. He wanted Miranda so much, he could barely breathe, and his wolf was nigh onto uncontrollable. It howled and snarled deep inside him. Garen forced it back. The last thing he needed was for fur or claws to sprout and ruin everything.

He could smell Miranda's lust with his enhanced senses. She was so aroused she was on the verge of coming. Strands of dark hair curled around her face. Her face was splotchy with excitement, and her blue eyes glowed warmly. Years of repressed desire slashed through him. He moved to the seat next to her and slid a hand between her legs. She moaned and pressed into him, but not before she yanked her headset out of the way and thumbed it to the off position.

Possessiveness sounded an exultant note behind his breastbone. She wasn't going to fight him. She wanted him just as much as he wanted her. He lowered his head and covered her mouth with his. She opened hers and sucked hungrily on his tongue. His cock throbbed. She wasn't the only one on the verge of coming.

He felt her fingers on the fastenings of his pants, and then her hands closed around his shaft. He wanted to do everything to her. Kiss her, lick her, suckle her incredible breasts, and run his mouth down her body to settle on her clit. All those things would have to wait. What mattered now was getting inside her. He reached for her pants, delighted to find they had an elastic waistband.

The logical part of his brain was nearly obliterated with passion, but it reminded him she needed at least one leg free, which meant one shoe off. Reluctantly, he broke away from their embrace and pried her fingers off his cock.

"What?" Her voice was muzzy with need. "You started this. Come back here, goddammit."

He laughed. God, it felt good to laugh and hold Miranda in his arms. "Patience, darling. I just need to get one of your pant legs out of the way. Then you can straddle me."

Between the two of them, they managed to unlace a boot and jimmy one of her legs out of her pants. He folded the chairs' armrests out of the way, settled his hands on her hips, and helped her kneel above him. When she lowered herself so the heat of her surrounded him, he gasped. Sensation so intense it set every nerve on fire lanced through him. Her muscles clenched around his cock and held on. Hard nipples pressed against his chest. He thrust upward, and his balls tightened.

"Sorry, darling. I'm not going to last long." He moved a hand between them and rubbed her swollen clit.

"It's okay. Neither am I." She smiled, all heat and fire and lust.

Her muscles milked him, and she sank her teeth into his shoulder. He could tell from her rhythmic movements and the tension in her nub that she was coming. Garen let himself go. He'd imagined coming inside Miranda forever, and now it was finally happening. He growled low in the back of his throat as semen arced into her.

He moved his hands to the sides of her face and kissed her long and deep. She turned her head, captured the fingers that had just been rubbing her, and licked them clean. It was so erotic, his cock throbbed where it was still buried deep in her pussy.

She wriggled out of his grasp, reached for the napkin wrapped around the beer bottle, and stuffed it between her legs before she pulled her underwear and pants back into place. Her face was a gorgeous, rosy hue. He started to tell her how lovely she was when she said, "Sorry. I'm sorry about that. Didn't mean to. You're my boss. I understand what we did was wrong. Don't worry, I won't let my, uh, my…well, whatever it was, get out of control again. I'm going into the head to clean up. We should probably have used a condom. I have an IUD, but still—"

"Whoa." He held up a hand, having a hard time with the transition from sexual high to a *we-shouldn't-have-done-this* conversation. "I enjoyed making love with you, Miranda. You're an amazing—"

She shook her head. "No. It was a mistake. It won't happen again. I promise. You caught me at a weak moment." She pushed past him and headed for the rear of the aircraft.

Garen shoved his still half-hard cock back into his pants and zipped up. A leaden deadness settled around his heart. She may have had sex with him, but Miranda didn't care about him. The post-coital conversation he hoped they'd have was considerably different. Sex had almost been mate bond intense, as was his longing for her. He wanted to tell her that, ask if she was a shifter…

He bit down hard on his disappointment. Better if he went back to the cockpit. That way she wouldn't have to look at him when she came back from the john.

And he wouldn't have to face her.

What could they possibly say to one another, beyond him apologizing for being swept off his feet by her lithe body and firm curves? No way could he tell her he truly cared about her. Not in light of the revulsion he'd seen mirrored in her face as she stammered through regrets. She was obviously appalled by what she considered a weakness.

So much for my mate bond theory.

Garen picked up his headset and settled it into place before walking into the cockpit. He wasn't certain just what he'd say to Lars. No way he'd be able to hide the lingering scent of sex. He latched the door and sat heavily. For a time neither of them said anything. Garen almost started to believe he could escape a conversation he'd assumed was inevitable.

"I do not like to pry, but I could smell sex even through the door." Lars glanced at Garen with a knowing grin on his face. "How was she?"

Garen gritted his teeth. "Hot, passionate, delectable." He inhaled, the air almost painful in his lungs. "But she doesn't care about me. Said I caught her at a weak moment. Apologized all over the place and said it would never happen again."

"It would be untrue if I said I was sorry." Lars flicked the front of his pants. "Imagining the two of you fucking got me going. I will need to take care of myself before I escort the fair *fraulein* anywhere." A hesitation. "I do not suppose there is any possibility the three of us could—"

"No." Something about the vehemence in Garen's tone earned him a penetrating look from Lars.

"Why not? It is not as if you are mated—"

"Get out of here. I'm done talking about this."

Lars shot a penetrating look his way. "Your airplane, my friend. I will be back."

"Miranda couldn't wait to get away from me. She might not be done in the head."

"If she is not, I will wait. Unless you wish to watch me masturbate." Lars winked lewdly.

"In a pig's eye. Go." Garen waved both hands at Lars. "It's a good thing we're friends. My tolerance for perverts is pretty limited."

"You know you love me." Lars blew a kiss and exited the cockpit.

To distract himself, Garen checked the instrument panel and their course line. He made a few calculations on the in-flight computer and estimated they'd be landing in roughly twenty-five minutes. He radioed the tower with their arrival time.

Because the airplane didn't really need his attention, his thoughts returned to Miranda—and to Roulan and ISL, his international human trafficking ring. Getting rid of Derek Roulan was a start, but it would take far more than that to break up his organization. Despite years of research that hadn't turned up much, Garen was convinced he'd only seen the tip of that iceberg. Set up by pros, the organization had deep claws in nearly every country—including the United States. Of course they had a much easier go in places like Asia, where young girls came cheap and parents were much less likely to report disappearances to the authorities.

Miranda.

He shut his eyes for a moment. He wasn't sure what had gotten into him. He'd managed to keep his hands off her for a very long time. What was different about today? Was it that she'd almost died? Or was it because Lars was interested in her, and Garen's wolf pushed him to stake a claim, so she'd be his and his alone? He'd been a fool to believe she was a potential mate. The mate bond wasn't limited to single candidates, but still the possibilities were few and far between.

No. If the mate bond were in play, she might've been uncomfortable after they made love, but she'd never have gone through that whole business about working for him and it never happening again.

"It doesn't matter." His words were low and bitter. "I botched things. Should've taken her out to a nice dinner. Courted her…"

Oh, really? an inner voice inquired drily. *And how was I going to do that? She works for me. I don't date employees. It's a violation of—*

He clamped a lid on his thoughts. Irritation simmered just below the surface. He'd painted himself into a corner, and he didn't see any way out. Garen prided himself on a cool, rational collectedness. It had pulled him through situations that would've been the death of lesser men. He'd survived despite his hot-headed wolf side and beaten the odds.

"*Bullshit*," his wolf, who rarely said anything, snarled. "*We survived because of me.*"

"Right," Garen snarled back. "You were a great help at the last shifter gathering. I think you mated with half the females there."

"*I would've had all of them if you hadn't called me off.*"

Garen bit back a wry laugh. He and the wolf were two sides of the same coin. It would be foolhardy to jeopardize everything he'd built so carefully in the human world just because his dick was out of control.

The cockpit door clicked open. Lars, looking a bit flushed, settled into his seat.

Garen quirked a brow. "Well, how were you?"

"Same as always. My hand is reliable."

Garen waited, but Lars didn't say anything further. Finally, he couldn't stand it. "How did Miranda seem?"

"I wondered if you were going to ask. My airplane. I will set us up on long final."

"I already radioed the tower, but it wouldn't hurt to give them an updated ETA. You didn't answer my question."

Lars shrugged. "She appeared tired. We did not talk."

A spurt of relief surged through him. *Good.* Miranda wasn't running to Lars with her problems. Garen set his jaw in a tense line. He still saw Miranda as his.

I'm going to have to get over that. Not only isn't she mine now. She never was.

"*She could be if you put a bit of effort into it,*" the wolf informed him tartly.

Garen didn't bother to answer.

Miranda stood on the tarmac, bag slung over her shoulder. The men's bags were next to her feet. Lars was turning the plane in, and Garen was securing a rental car. Thank fucking God neither man seemed particularly inclined toward conversation. Embarrassment heated her face. She was certain the men had discussed her sexual lapse. After what Lars had told her about the depth of their relationship, it was nearly impossible they hadn't talked about it.

I can't go back. All I can do is hold my head up and get through this somehow.

It worried her that Lars would label her and assume bedding her was a foregone conclusion. The more she thought about it, the less she wanted him to stay with her. She craved her wolf form. Once in it, she'd spend the next week running wild in the Pacific Northwest's forests. By the time she resurfaced, her side would be healed—and so would her mind. Maybe not her heart, but two out of three wasn't bad.

A black Lincoln Navigator rolled up next to her. Garen jumped out and tossed his and Lars' bags into the boot. He held out a hand for hers. She handed it to him and got into the back seat.

"Don't you want to sit up front?"

She shook her head, not totally trusting herself to speak. Lars strode into view. She released a tightly held breath. As uncomfortable as things were with the three of them, it was worse with just her and Garen. Lars settled in the passenger seat. Garen got behind the wheel and asked, "Would anyone like anything before we leave Bellingham?"

"Food would be welcome," Lars said.

"Sure," she said. "Something quick. We can eat while we drive."

"Easy for you to say," Garen murmured.

"I can drive while you eat, and then we could trade," she offered.

"Nah. I was just teasing. How do burgers sound?"

Lars made a face. She saw it in the rearview mirror. "Americans," he muttered. "Your appetites are so banal."

"The last chicken burger I ate in Munich had bones in it," Garen sniped.

"That is because the Germans are still trying to rid themselves of American trash."

Miranda rolled her eyes, grateful the men were bantering back and forth.

She ordered fries, a cheeseburger, and a vanilla shake at a small drive-in. Part of her wanted Coke, but the shake had more calories, and she figured she needed fuel. "So," she said around a mouthful of meat, cheese, and mayonnaise. "About that safe house in the countryside."

"Are you certain it's what you want?" Garen asked.

"If a hotel does not meet your tastes," Lars added, "it would be easy to move you to another. The presence of crowds would mask our movements."

"I'm sure," she said and sucked some shake through a straw. "I still prefer the forest. After all, it's not forever. How long will I be invisible? A week? Ten days?"

"At least a week," Garen said. "Maybe longer. I need to test the waters after I'm back at HQ. If we can bring you out of hiding earlier, we will."

Alarm bells sounded in her brain. "I will have a say in this, won't I? You might decide it isn't safe a month from now. I have no intention of burying myself forever."

"Even if it means your life?" Lars asked. His voice held a hard edge she hadn't heard before.

"Being locked away is a lot like being dead."

Garen blew out a breath, the sound loud in the confines of the car. "We have three locations between here and the greater Seattle area. The most remote is up Highway 2. The mountains behind Index are rugged. Very few venture into that area, who aren't locals —"

"—so if I keep my eyes open, I should be able to recognize people who have no business there," she finished for him.

"Exactly."

"Will you get me a new phone?"

"Once you return to work."

She ate a couple of fries. "Probably wouldn't work out there anyway—unless it was a sat phone."

"You're getting ahead of yourself, Miss Miller. Once you're fully vetted, Rubicon International will get you a sat phone. Not before."

"Sorry." *Christ. I'm forever apologizing to that man.* "Since I can't use my phone, are my credit cards are off-limits as well?"

"Good thinking," Garen said. "I'll see you're adequately provisioned. Your Jayne Powers ID hasn't been compromised—"

"Perhaps not the name," Lars interrupted, "but the ISL gang knows what she looks like now. I am certain they would have a way to access passport photos for arrivals and departures from the country."

"Point taken. All right, the Powers ID is off the table. You can hand it over once we reach our destination. We'll stop at a pharmacy. Get yourself some red hair dye. I'll have Jorge make you up new ID docs and credit cards. Someone will deliver them in the next day or so. In the meantime, you can get by on cash. Anyway, the house should be fully stocked."

"Um, boss, it's not easy to turn hair as dark as mine red unless I bleach it first. How about if I get one of those frost kits. I'll make it really blonde in the front, and I'll cut a bunch off."

"I can help with that," Lars offered smoothly.

"Just one more talent, right along with flying and killing and paramedic-ing?" Miranda clapped a hand to her forehead. "Sorry. My mouth gets ahead of my brain sometimes."

Lars chuckled. "I have found it useful to disguise both myself and others, so yes, you could describe it as another talent."

She sank back against the leather seat of the Lincoln and finished her meal. She didn't really want Lars to stay with her but couldn't think of a diplomatic way to refuse him, particularly since she'd accepted his offer earlier.

What do I want?

The answer came back so fast, her mind reeled. *Garen.* She

wanted more of Garen. The tiny bit she'd had was nowhere near enough. The reality of his hands and mouth and cock was ever so much better than they'd been in her imagination. They'd torn at each other like animals and come almost before they'd gotten started. Not quite the romantic interlude she'd imagined all the times she brought herself off with him in her mind.

Not romantic at all, her inner voice intruded. *What happened in the Learjet was sex, pure and simple. I was already hot when he sat across from me. Men sense things like that, and it takes less than nothing to get them going. If I were smart, I'd forget all about having fucked him and move on.*

Problem was, she didn't want to. She'd do almost anything to have the hard, well-muscled planes of his body jammed up against her again. Miranda shook her head.

Got to get hold of myself, or I'll fall into his arms the next time he so much as looks at me.

She refocused her mental energy. It was obvious she'd have to hang around the safe house at least long enough for her new ID to arrive. So much for burying herself in the woods and letting her wolf take over for a while. Miranda swallowed. She didn't like it when other people called the shots. It had been one of the worst aspects of the military. Lost in her thoughts, she was surprised when the car jolted to a stop.

She glanced out the window. A shopping center. She started to get out of the car, but Garen swung around and grabbed her arm. "Where do you think you're going?"

"To get hair dye."

"I'll do that. The store probably has cameras. You don't want to be caught on tape or film anywhere." He shook her slightly. "I trained you better than that."

"No," she muttered. "The U.S. Army did." She dragged her legs inside the car.

Garen shoved her door shut and took off at a trot for Rite Aid.

She and Lars sat in silence for several minutes before he said, "It will not be as bad as you believe, *fraulein*. The days will pass quickly. I am certain we shall find ways to—"

"That's just it." She dove into the breach. *In for a penny, in for a pound.* "While it was very kind of you to offer, I really would rather be alone."

Lars turned in his seat and met her gaze. "I would not do anything you did not want me to."

"I'm sure you wouldn't." She tried to smile. "I, um, I live by myself. I'm used to being alone. It's bad enough I can't go home..." Miranda let her words trail off and hoped like hell he wouldn't make this harder than it already was.

"I understand, *fraulein*. More than you think. I will stay until your new ID shows up. If I remember correctly, the safe house has many bedrooms. Do not worry. I will give you adequate privacy."

"It's really not necessary."

"Oh, but I think it is." Garen let himself into the car and tossed a paper bag into the back seat. "Take a quick look and tell me if it's what you wanted."

She peeked into the bag and rolled it back up. "Yeah, this will work fine. How could you possibly know what we were talking about?"

"I have very good hearing. One of us will stay with you until your ID arrives. Your only choice, Miss Miller, is which one."

She nodded. Resignation—never a good feeling—sat heavy in her gut. The thing she didn't understand was Garen. He was positively chipper, a vast departure from his demeanor ever since she'd made the error of letting her hormones rule her common sense.

Christ! He was actually whistling as he nosed the car out of the huge parking lot and turned onto Highway 2.

Maybe I'll tell both of them to stay. That way they can entertain each other, and they'll leave me alone.

Garen watched the Lincoln roll out of the long driveway with Lars at the wheel. He glanced around a clearing hogged out of a forest thick with evergreens. A two-story cabin sat a quarter mile back from the logging road that provided access to it. A brook babbled crisply down from one of many steep ravines lining the central Cascades. The beauty of this location was its relative remoteness. A bevy of sensors kicked off silent alarms in the house if anything broke multiple beams across the turnoff from the logging road.

He took the steps into the house two at a time. Miranda had disappeared inside with her bag within seconds of their arrival. The edges of his mouth twitched, lost somewhere between amusement and concern. She'd been so intent on getting away from both him and Lars, she'd nearly run through the heavy, metal-reinforced door. He'd joined her on the porch to activate the electronics to unlock it. Despite her eagerness to get into the house, she'd shied away from him, making it obvious his touch wasn't welcome.

He let himself inside and shut the door. Built of logs, the cabin blended nicely into the surrounding forest. The lower floor was one large room. A substantial woodstove had been plumbed into one end of it, with a stack of split wood laying on one side of the hearth. The cabin ran on solar—a dicey proposition with all the evergreens around the house—and a backup generator, so the woodstove was more than decorative.

Garen clamped his jaws together in frustration. Women. He had no idea what had changed between when Miranda nudged her pussy into his hand and welcomed him inside her body and now. If looks could kill, he'd be deader than the spider corpses he swept out of the way as he pulled dustcovers off the furniture.

He upended his computer bag on the round, oak table and fiddled with the setup to hook his laptop to a scrambled satellite link. He needed access to his desktop at Rubicon International. He also wanted to get Miranda's new documentation in process. He grimaced. She hadn't liked being backed into a corner. He'd seen anger and resentment smolder in her blue eyes when he told her it was a waste of manpower for both him and Lars to remain.

That was when she'd muttered, "Fine," set her mouth in a hard line, and scampered into the house.

After a private conference with the European branch of RI, Lars was en route to Spokane. From there, he'd fly himself back to Europe in stages, unless some black ops were in process stateside.

As a parting shot to Garen, Lars had said, "Good luck, my friend. She has a temper, and at the moment she is furious." His austere features had brightened into a warm smile. "Still, if I had my way, we would trade problems. Taming spitfires is right up my alley."

Garen rolled his eyes and booted up his computer. He wasn't planning to tame Miranda. Simply getting along with her for the next twenty-four to thirty-six hours until he could escape and nurse his wounded feelings in private might prove beyond him. His cock was giving him nothing but grief. It had been hard ever since he'd induced Miranda to join the Mile High Club.

Wonder if she even knows what that is?

He rearranged himself, but it didn't help much. His zipper still dug into his engorged flesh. It was agony sitting at the table, knowing she was so close. For fuck's sake, he could smell her, all musk and lavender and something unique to Miranda. His wolf was on the prowl, which didn't make things any easier. It wanted more of Miranda too. Garen couldn't remember it ever being so... enthusiastic about any of his women. His hand strayed back to his crotch, but he forced his fingers back to the keyboard. Even if he brought himself off, it wouldn't make a dent in his lust.

He wanted Miranda, but she didn't want him. Unused to indulging his emotions, Garen tried to push disappointment aside, but it bounced back stubbornly and slapped him in the face. He'd never let a woman get under his skin before. More to the point, he'd always been a fuck-'em-and-forget-'em type. What was it about this woman? It had to be more than working in close proximity. He'd been attracted to several of his agents in the past. He liked his women strong, capable, and independent. But he'd always managed to wait until the agents had tenure, and once he fucked them, that was that. He didn't want them anymore. He shook his head and attempted to refocus, but a persistent sadness lodged behind his breastbone.

Maybe it's karma. Some goddess with a sense of humor is getting back at me for all the hearts I've broken.

He bent to the task of typing in the coding to scramble his location and information. It took a while, but his desktop finally flared across the screen. Garen grimaced as he assessed the state of his inbox. Work. As usual, lots had piled up. The day, month, or season never mattered. Business was always brisk at Rubicon International.

Light was fading from the day when he finally looked up. The house was absolutely silent. The only thing that hadn't abated was Miranda's earthy scent. He flicked a switch. The light came on, but it was weak. He thought about firing the generator but was hesitant to break the soothing quiet of the forest. He pushed out of his chair and rotated his torso to get the kinks out before striding to the woodstove. When he tugged the doors open, he grinned. Some considerate agent had actually left a nice pile of scrunched up paper and kindling. He struck a match on the rough cast-iron stove casing and lit the pile of tinder, checking to be sure the damper was fully open.

Garen hunkered next to the stove for long enough to make certain the fire would go, feeding it at intervals. He straightened. Still no Miranda. He thought about hunting her down and then discarded the idea. She was an adult. She'd surface in her own time. Or not. In the meantime, his stomach constricted. Lunch had been hours ago.

Garen riffled through cupboards and finally settled on a box of scalloped potatoes and a can of tuna. He figured he'd mix the tuna with the potatoes. A package of cheesecake mix would make a most excellent dessert. He'd blend in some whiskey to give it a lift. He started with dessert to give it time to set. The cabin's appliances ran on propane, so the small refrigerator did its job in spades. If he remembered right, things froze in the refrigerator section and got so hard in the freezer, it took hours for them to thaw. He poured himself a mug of whiskey and sipped as he worked. Every once in a while he chucked more wood into the stove. When the cabin grew warm enough, he stripped to his shirtsleeves.

Miranda galloped to the upper floor of the cabin and peeked in all six rooms. Four were bedrooms, one a bath, and the last a conference room. She picked the room at the very end of the hall, mostly because it had a small balcony that looked out onto the forest. After chucking her bag onto a chair, she glanced around the room. The ceiling pitched steeply with dormer windows and balcony doors framed in. A double bed with a colorful quilt sat off to one side. An oak tallboy with a mirror over it and a small table with two chairs completed the room's furniture. The floor was bare wooden planks with throw rugs strategically placed.

She pushed the balcony doors open and inhaled deeply. The air smelled sweet and clean. Her lupine senses detected a rich bevy of rodents—all within easy striking distance—and another wolf or two, a few coyotes, and some mountain lions. The roar of the Lincoln's powerful motor and tires crunching over gravel told her Lars was leaving. The irritation she'd swallowed like a bitter draught when Garen had dismissed her suggestion about both of them staying rose to mock her. She'd never felt quite so powerless, and the whole thing pissed her off.

It's like I'm a little girl, and the menfolk decided what was best for me.

A muted snarl escaped her throat. Her wolf informed her it would be child's play to leap from the balcony and disappear into the forest. She pulled the door shut to lessen temptation. After pacing up and down the room until she almost couldn't stand herself, Miranda unlaced her boots, toed them off, and lay on the bed. Her mind was a confused jumble. The worst part should've been fear the ISL gang wasn't done with her. Instead, the thought that rose to the top over and over was how the hell she'd manage to keep to herself under the same roof with Garen.

As it was, the urge to hurtle downstairs and into his arms was nearly irresistible. She shut her eyes in a vain attempt to sleep. Garen's face formed behind her closed lids. He was lean, yet powerfully built with broad shoulders and a hard, flat stomach. Not that she'd seen all that much of his body. They'd barely undressed in the plane. She'd gotten conversant with his cock, though. What an amazing appendage. Long and thick, his ridged flesh had felt heaven-sent inside her. She wanted to lick the length of his heavy shaft and plant nibbling kisses around the head.

He had glorious hair. Black, shot with silver, it was thick and smelled delicious. Like bay rum and sandalwood. Miranda ran her hands down her body and snorted.

Yeah, maybe I should ask what kind of shampoo he uses, so my hair can smell like that too.

Like she'd done so many times before, she teased her body with practiced fingertips and pretended Garen's hands and mouth moved over her sensitive flesh. Somewhere between her second and third orgasms, she realized one of her biggest problems was she'd used Garen as a fantasy object since the first day she'd laid eyes on him. To have finally moved her dreams to reality was too much to deal with, let alone resist. He wanted her—maybe not as intensely as she wanted him—but she was certain he'd fuck her again if she came on to him.

Miranda pulled a hand from her crotch and the other from a nipple. She got to her feet and padded to the door, listening intently.

Good. I'm still alone up here.

She gathered the hair dye and a change of clothes from her bag—serviceable clothing, warm and not too formfitting—and skittered into the bathroom. A shower would be perfect to cool her overheated libido and wash off the sweat from travel.

The water was hot and plentiful, the towels fluffy. By the time she combed out her newly bleached hair, it was nearly dark outside. She slid into black combat pants and an oversized, long-sleeved wool shirt. It seemed chilly, so she layered a jacket over everything. Someone had left a pair of sheepskin slippers in the bathroom. She tried them on, pleasantly surprised that they fit.

When she opened the bathroom door, the smell of food cooking hit her in the face. Excellent, because she was hungry. Before she went off on a tangent daydreaming impossibilities—like a life with Garen—she smoothed her features into cool neutrality and walked downstairs, comb in hand. The next order of business would be cutting her newly-colored hair.

His back was toward her as he stood at the stove. It might've been her imagination, but she thought he stiffened before turning to face her. His smile was warm enough, though.

"I was wondering whether or not to come upstairs and tell you dinner was almost ready." His eyes widened. "Wow! You weren't kidding about a lot of blonde around your face."

"Too much?" She fingered the damp strands. It had come as a

shock to her too, when she'd glanced in the steamy bathroom mirror. The hair around her face was almost totally platinum with equally light streaks spreading through her dark tresses.

"No. It was just a surprise. I'm not sure why I thought you'd wait until tomorrow to take care of your hair."

"Is there a pair of scissors here?"

He nodded, yanked a drawer open, and pulled some out. "You have such beautiful hair. It's a shame to cut it, but I still think it's necessary. Sit over there. Did you bring a comb down with you? If not, I have one."

She held up a comb and waggled it at him. "What? You and Lars both double as beauticians?"

He favored her with a grin. "We're a full-service operation, ma'am."

"What about dinner? Does it need attention?"

Garen laughed. It was a rich, warm sound. She didn't know if she'd ever heard him laugh before. "Does everything that comes out of your mouth end with a question mark, woman?"

"You just asked one. I really can cut my own hair."

"Sit." He pointed at a chair. When she looked at the table, she saw papers strewn about a fancy-looking laptop with a seventeen-inch screen. He must've been working before he made their dinner.

"To answer one of your other questions—" he turned off the stove "—dinner will keep for the few minutes it takes to chop a foot or so off your hair."

She sat, laid her comb on the table, and steeled herself to resist his touch. It wasn't easy. He finger-combed her hair before stabilizing sections with the comb. Miranda aimed for a normal respiration rate, but it was damn near impossible with him so close. Her nipples hardened. Despite her upstairs orgasms, her clit swelled with need, and liquid dribbled into her fresh pair of panties.

"There," he said with an odd catch in his voice and cleared his throat. "That should do it. We'll know more once it dries. I'll just get the broom and sweep up the mess."

"I can do that." She jumped to her feet and almost ran headlong into him. "You, uh, figure out what we need for supper since you know where things are."

His face looked flushed, but the light in the cabin was dim. She tried not to look, but her eyes strayed to his crotch. The distinctive swell of an erection thrilled her. To keep herself from dive-bombing his cock, she hurried across the kitchen and tugged open what looked like a utility closet. She was rewarded by brooms, buckets, and dustpans. Miranda grabbed what she needed and hustled back to the table to sweep up her hair.

Her head felt pounds lighter. She glanced at the pile on the floor and understood he'd cut her tresses to shoulder length. She probably should've cut it years ago. Hair as long as hers was a liability in the field, but she'd loved her lush locks and resisted everyone, from the aunt who raised her to her Army field lieutenant, when they told her to cut her hair. Garen had accomplished the impossible, but she didn't say a word.

By the time she'd dumped the bin and put everything away in the utility closet, he'd dished up their meal, and it waited on the table. "Would you like something to drink?" he asked.

"What are my choices?"

"There's a pretty good liquor cabinet here. Name your poison." Like her, he seemed to have regained his equanimity.

She blew out a breath. Maybe they'd manage better than she thought keeping their hands off one another. "Single malt scotch or Irish whiskey."

"We have both."

"Okay, I'll take the scotch." She looked around for a stash of bottles.

"I'll bring it to the table. Sit and eat before everything gets cold."

She tucked into the potato and tuna casserole. It was surprisingly good. When he handed her a mug of scotch, she took an experimental sip. The liquor burned a path down her throat to her stomach, warming her. "Thanks."

"You're welcome." He slid into the place opposite her and closed his computer, moving it to the side.

"Any news from the outside world?" She gestured at the laptop with her fork.

"Nothing about ISL, if that's what you mean. Your new ID is in process. I told Jorge to make you mostly blonde with shoulder-length hair and to sort of fuzz out your sharp cheekbones."

"Do you suppose Lars is all right?"

Garen shot her an odd look. "He ought to be. He's been taking care of himself for a very long time. He called from the Spokane airport. He was waiting for either a Learjet or a Gulfstream with enough range to take him back to Boston without stopping to refuel. From there, I'm not certain." A hesitation. "Why? Do you miss him? Are you sorry it's me here and not him?"

Her eyes widened, and her heart beat a little faster. For a moment, Garen had sounded like a jealous lover.

Don't be absurd. He's used to running the show, that's all.

"Now who's asking the questions?" She kept her tone light. "I didn't mean anything by it. I was just making conversation."

He chewed and swallowed, and then took a long draught of whatever was in his own mug. "Of course. I'm sorry. I shouldn't have asked. Tell me about yourself, Miranda."

"Huh? But you already know nearly everything about me from the application I filled out to work for Rubicon International." She muffled a snort. "I have to say, it was the most thorough job application I've ever seen."

He knitted his brows together. "Tell me anyway, Miss Miller. You've worked for Rubicon International for five years, give or take. I have an excellent memory, but it doesn't extend to job applications I looked at quite so far back."

"How about if you tell me about yourself?" she countered. "I know next to nothing about you." Miranda captured her lower lip in her teeth, amazed she'd been so gutsy.

"I can do that, so long as you return the favor. Shall we play a version of I'll show you mine, if you show me yours?"

The bantering undertone in his words caught her by surprise. If Garen had a playful side, she'd never seen it. "Sure. I'll even go first. I grew up in Portland. Both my parents were killed in a bad automobile accident when I was four, so I went to live with an aunt in Mount Shasta. Graduated high school and went to UCSF. Got a degree in criminal justice, joined the Army, and ended up in the Berets. No husbands. No kids." Miranda slapped her palms together a time or two. "Your turn."

He chuckled. "Your Green Beret training is showing. I'm not certain I've ever heard a more concise encapsulation of close to thirty years. Let's see if I can top it. My parents are still alive. They're in Lausanne, Switzerland. No brothers or sisters. I went to Cambridge. Majored in archeology. Got sucked into the British Secret Intelligence Services, MI6, and started Rubicon International a few years later." He mimicked her hand slapping gesture.

She furled her brows. "Wives? Kids?"

The corners of his mouth twitched. "Why, Miss Miller, how forward of you. I don't have to answer you, but I will. Neither—on both fronts."

To mask the joy sluicing through her about Garen's unattached status, she moved the serving dish closer. There were a few spoonfuls left. "Do you want more?"

He shook his head. "Save room for dessert. We have cheesecake laced with whiskey."

"Never fear, I can eat this and that too." Since he didn't want any more, she gobbled the rest of the potato casserole out of the pot and chased it with the last of her scotch.

He got to his feet. "I'll grab dessert. Would you like another shot of scotch?"

She rolled her eyes. "Let's wait to see how much whiskey you dumped in the cheesecake."

His blue eyes danced with suppressed glee. "Should I take exception to that? Most women have found me a credible cook."

At least none of them was your wife.

"Don't take exception. Thanks for making supper for us. I truly appreciate it." Miranda felt her cheeks heat and clamped down on her thoughts. Maybe one mug of liquor would do it for her.

The cheesecake was delectable—rich and smooth with just the right amount of bite from the whiskey. She'd worked her way through about half of a generous slice when a bank of lights flashed off and on over the stove. "What the hell? Are we having a power outage?"

"No." His voice was sharp, and he sounded like the old Garen, the one she knew from work. "We're having company. Damn it. Run upstairs and get whichever of your guns holds the most ammo. Bring an extra clip."

"Maybe we should stay upstairs." She kept her voice low. "Two of the rooms have balconies."

"Not a bad idea. I'm hoping they won't get that far."

She opened her mouth to question him. He waved her to silence. "Go get your gun. Do it now."

Recognizing a command when she heard it, Miranda hightailed it up the stairs.

CHAPTER 7

Garen counted to himself. When he was almost certain whoever was headed their way would cross the land-mined strip farthest from the house, he depressed a plunger in the front closet and was rewarded with a distant boom. Part of him was angry to be back in work mode. He'd been enjoying his dinner and conversation with Miranda more than he'd enjoyed anything in a very long time. She had a razor-sharp mind. In tandem with her perfect body, it created a very enticing package.

Back off. She works for me.

I could fire her.

Yes, but then I'd have to marry her.

He nearly laughed aloud. Would have if they weren't under attack. He watched the lights mounted over the kitchen sink. They'd flash if the intruders breached the next beam. In all, there were three points that kicked off alarms. He mouthed a silent prayer of thanks that the storage batteries—deep cycle marine—had held enough juice to warn him.

Miranda moved to his side, silent as a wraith, her 9mm semiautomatic clutched in one hand. He glanced down and noted she'd traded her slippers for boots. *Good girl.* She raised a questioning eyebrow. He shook his head. "Watch the lights over the sink."

"I thought they were over the stove."

"There are three sets. For once in your life, do what I tell you without asking a bunch of questions. I'm surprised the Berets didn't throw you out."

She smirked. "Yeah, at the time it surprised me too. Should we kill the lights?"

"Nah. They know we're here."

"Do you have a plan?"

"Several." The light bank over the sink flashed. "Damn! Means at least some of them got through the first set of land mines." He dove for the closet and set off the next group of explosives. Much closer, they rocked the house and lit up the windows.

"What? Hundred fifty yards?"

"You're good."

"It's why I'm still alive. If the first round of mined explosives was that potent, it probably means there are a lot of ISL people out there. Do you think we should take to the woods? We'd have more maneuverability."

Garen considered it. The crash of breaking glass made up his mind. He scooped the grenade off the floor and heaved it back through the window it had hurtled through. Nanoseconds later, an explosion nearly deafened him. "We don't have a choice," he snapped. "Fade out one of the back windows. Stay behind the house."

"Com devices?"

"Don't have any. Miranda—"

She pulled her jacket hood over her bright hair and cinched it. "Boss?"

"Don't get yourself killed."

"I don't intend to."

He gathered a Kalashnikov from the front closet, slapped a high-capacity clip into it, and dropped two more into a pocket. For good measure, he detonated the last set of land mines. The blast rocked the house and pummeled his sensitive hearing. Maybe it would kill a few more of the bastards. He wasn't certain he'd need the assault rifle. His wolf form was better for some things, but it was best to be prepared for anything. He dialed in his lupine senses and listened intently. Nothing. Maybe the last blast had done it.

Garen slipped out the ground-level window Miranda had used and flattened himself against the rough-hewn logs of the cabin. The only thing he could smell was explosive residue. His ears still rang from the series of blasts. He grabbed a handful of dirt and smeared his face before pulling his own hood over his head.

The forest wasn't far. Maybe twenty yards. Their best bet would be for him to lose himself among the trees and circle the house to gather intel about their attackers. Problem was, if the ISL thugs had any brains, they'd be doing the same thing. He made his way to thick tree cover as he considered his options. A bullet zipped past, followed by another. Senses on high alert, he moved deeper into the woods. His nose twitched; he picked out several different human scents, counting as he went. Eight. Not so bad, but where was Miranda? Her scent should've stood out, but it simply wasn't there.

Fear bit deep that the bastards had killed her, but he batted it aside. Even if she were dead, he'd still smell her. She was a skilled agent. There was some good reason he couldn't scent her presence...

A branch crackled. He fired and heard a muted scream. Someone jumped him from behind. The force drove both of them to the ground. His gun was useless, squashed between his body and the damp loam of the forest floor. A gun barrel jammed against his skull.

"Where is the woman?"

"What woman?" Garen tried to jackknife his body from under his assailant. It was like trying to move a ton of bricks.

"I am holding a gun to your head," the Slovakian-accented voice continued.

"Tell me something I don't know."

"The woman." The gun prodded harder.

"What woman? There are so many in my life."

"Very funny, wiseass."

Boots crashed through the thick undergrowth. A spray of Eastern European language went back and forth. While the man who had him pinned wasn't totally focused on him, Garen twisted hard. He gave it all he had and butted the man in the groin with the side of his head. His assailant grunted in surprise and pain. Before the second jerk got his wits together, Garen yanked his body free, levered the Kalashnikov out from beneath him, and pointed it. The beauty of assault rifles was you didn't need to aim. He pulled the trigger, and both men went down in a spray of blood and bullets.

He bolted to his feet and wiped gore out of his eyes. Voices reached him from the front of the house. It sounded as if reinforcements had arrived from somewhere. It made sense they would've been in contact with backup thugs. Garen bit down hard. Where the fuck was Miranda? He'd have sold his soul for com devices.

Rather than heading for a certain confrontation, he faded back into the trees. "Miranda." He kept his voice barely there. "Where are you?" He didn't see where she came from, but she materialized out of the darkness, smelling of blood. He hoped to Christ it wasn't hers. "Are you hurt?"

"No. I was getting ready to kill that jackal who had you pinned. Had a little mess of my own to get out of first."

"How many down?" Breath whooshed out of him. He sent up prayers to every deity imaginable that she was still alive. He wanted to wrap his arms around her and draw her close, but he held himself back. Now wasn't the time.

"Three. Caught 'em heading for the back door with a pile of grenades."

He would've whistled but didn't want to make any more noise than necessary. "I'm betting you know where the explosives are."

"Follow me." She disappeared into the trees and led him to a neat stack of ten grenades. She stuffed four into her pockets and hefted a fifth in the hand not carrying her gun.

"How you doing for ammo?" He picked up the rest of the grenades.

"All right—" The night came alive with light and the sound of shattering glass. She made a huffing sound. "Good thing I put on warm clothes. Looks as if the place will probably burn to the ground before they're done."

"Maybe not. Depends how intent they are on finding you. It takes time to set a good enough fire to burn a building that size to cinders."

She shrugged. "Grenades do a fair job. What's next? I heard reinforcements drive up."

He snapped his sat phone from a pocket, keyed in a code, and terminated the connection. "The cavalry will arrive as soon as they can get a couple of choppers in the air."

"I meant in the meantime." Annoyance dripped from her tone. "That will take an hour."

"Forty minutes."

"Regardless."

He inhaled raggedly. Time to take a chance. He spun her to face him, put his hands on her shoulders, and spoke right into her ear. "We could spend the time lobbing death back and forth—and maybe get hurt because the odds aren't great. Or I can take a different form where it will be easier to protect you. I'm a wolf shifter—"

Shock ratcheted through him when she hugged him, drew back, and slid out of her clothes. Then he understood what she was doing. Damn if Lars hadn't been right about her. He wondered what animal she'd be. In seconds a gorgeous black and gray timber wolf nudged him with her snout.

"What are you waiting for?" Her voice resonated in his mind.

Good question. He grabbed her clothes and gun and trotted deeper into the forest. When the going became nearly impossible, at least in his human form, he dumped everything in a hollowed out tree and shucked his own garments, wrapping them around the rifle and sidearm to keep the damp out.

Gunfire and the boom of grenades followed them right along with men yelling in the guttural Slovakian language he didn't understand. Miranda loped back toward the thick of things.

"What are you doing?" he called after her.

"Maybe I can pick off a few, if they separate from the rest."

Her mind voice echoed with feral overtones. His wolf side grinned and would've howled, but he muffled it. How the hell had she hidden her dual nature from the U.S. Army? The woman must have incredible control. He flanked her. Now that she'd brought it up, killing some of the bastards in an up close and personal way with his teeth sounded like great sport.

Miranda stalked one of the men, so silent on her thickly padded feet he never knew what hit him until she launched herself and buried her teeth in his neck. Garen didn't think it accidental she'd picked the side with the man's com device or that she obliterated the plastic tubing in her jaws right along with his carotid artery. Normally, he'd have wanted one of the devices to listen in on the enemy. Not much point since he didn't understand their language.

He watched Miranda, paws splayed on either side of her victim. He'd never seen her work before—in any form. Other businesses like his frequently deployed agents in pairs or trios, but he'd always preferred to work alone, so he made his agents do the same. It built creativity and guts if operatives had to solve their problems with brains and courage—plus whatever they'd either brought with them or managed to filch or fashion in the field. Rubicon International had a much lower ratio of agents who signed on to agents who finished training than any other outfit, but Garen believed he gained a significantly higher quality of employee as a result.

Miranda sashayed to his side. Garen couldn't help himself. He licked blood off her snout. She licked him back and leaned into him, rubbing the side of her head against him. His wolf's cock swelled within its furred sheath. If it weren't so dangerous, he wanted nothing more than to claim her and sink inside her hot, wet folds. The bulb at the base of his cock would seal them together for long minutes—maybe as much as half an hour. During that time they'd be helpless. Reluctantly, he pulled away.

"*Let's see if we can find another.*" She tilted her head to one side and eyed him. "*You look awfully familiar.*"

"*I should,*" he growled. "*I'm your boss.*" Garen blew air through his nostrils. Damn it. He'd hoped for anonymity. Should've known better.

She's too good an agent not to be on top of something as simple as this.

"*Not what I meant,*" Miranda persisted.

Garen had to divert her before she figured things out. No one knew he was Lucifer. Things had to stay that way to maintain the gains he'd made for lycans. The old saying about the only way two people can keep a secret is if one of them is dead bounced around his head, and he chided himself for being a risk-taking fool. He had no intention of killing the woman he was falling hard for, so he had to sidetrack her.

"*Look sharp. We can pick off a couple more. I'll take the guy on the right.*" Garen trailed his prey and leapt at the last minute. Blood— hot, salty, and smelling of copper—slid down his throat, and he lost himself in the joy of the kill.

He had to reclaim his human form before Miranda, with the instincts of a bloodhound, uncovered his secret. Of course he'd look familiar. He'd presided over the lycan group at every shifter gathering for the past several years. Fortunately, his pelt was about the same color as most of the other lycans, and she'd never gotten close enough to scent him. Thank God, she wasn't one of the many he'd mated with. Beyond the first flush of his excitement at discovering she was a shifter just like him, the reality of what it meant came crashing down. Why couldn't she have been some other species? It would've made his life ever so much easier.

He kept his identities scrupulously separate. No one except Lars knew that the head of Rubicon International was also the lycan leader, and he meant to keep it that way. For that fact, outside the inner cadre of RI, no one knew he was lycan. His status in the international spy community would crash and burn if his secret became known.

Garen left his kill long before he wanted to and made his way to where he'd left their clothes. Reinforcements would arrive soon. He and Miranda would be fine as humans again. He wasn't worried about her divulging his lycan side. After all, he had the goods on her too, but he couldn't let their relationship go any further. She'd want to shift and run with him, and he couldn't let that happen. If she saw him in wolf form under any kind of light, she'd know him for who he was.

He was dressed by the time she made her way to his side. *"I wondered what happened to you,"* she said.

He used his mind voice since she was still in her lycan form. *"The troops will be here soon. I'll turn around and give you some privacy."*

~

WHAT IF I don't want privacy?

She'd been feeling pretty high. Adrenaline and killing bad guys always gave her a rush. Garen wolf-kissing her nose had been mighty incredible too. She'd hoped for more lupine foreplay, but here he was human again. And offering to turn around to boot. She would've liked it better if he'd ogled her while she got her clothes back on. The distant *thump-thump* of rotors told her Garen's estimate had been spot on. She shifted and dressed.

"It's safe to turn around now." She tried to keep the acid—and the hurt—out of her voice, but failed.

Spotlights from the choppers brightened the moonless night. She saw his face clearly. It was a study in ambivalence. "We'll talk, but not now. Check your gun. Make certain—"

"I know all that, Daddy."

What am I doing? I work for him, and I just sounded insubordinate as hell.

"Sorry," she added quickly. "Don't mind me. Not enough sleep. Thanks for looking out for me."

Weapon fire blatted as the choppers strafed men on the ground. Garen pulled his sat phone out and spoke into it, his voice low and urgent. She supposed he was relaying their position. It'd be a bitch to be killed by friendly fire.

Miranda wasn't sure what tipped her off. Maybe her lupine senses were still close to the surface. She spun so her back was to Garen and fired. He shoved her out of the way and sprayed the forest with rounds from his Kalashnikov. A heaving grunt told her someone's bullet—likely Garen's—had found its target.

Something wasn't right. How had one of the enemy tracked them to their remote corner of the woods? She glanced at Garen. "You just killed a shifter."

"I already figured that out. Want to go see what he was?"

She sent her enhanced senses ahead. Whoever was there had tracked them on his own. Though not quite dead yet, it was inevitable given the stench of a gut shot. Miranda shook herself back to here and now. However disappointed she felt about Garen's sudden change of heart toward her, her unhappiness had no place in the field. Agents who indulged in emotions got killed.

She worked her way forward cautiously. Animals in their death throes could do a lot of damage. A bear lay on its side, flanks heaving. Blood bubbled out its mouth.

"I know you can hear me. Finish what you began." The bear's mind voice was low and rumbly, with the same Eastern European accent.

"All right. Mercy in exchange for information." She wondered how he could possibly know she was a shifter but left it alone for now. If there was time, she'd ask.

The bear's small eyes narrowed. *"Maybe. It depends what you want to know."*

"Where is the main ISL shop here in the U.S?"

"San Diego."

"How do I know you're telling me the truth?"

More blood burbled past his lips, staining his dark brown coat. *"What more do I have to lose?"*

"How did you know I was—er, that I'd be able to hear your mind voice?"

He grunted in pain and shifted his bulk a little. *"We received intel about you after you eliminated Roulan. Secrets like that are hard to keep—if you flaunt your animal side. Please."* His breath came in little panting gasps. *"I have done as you requested."*

She raised her pistol and hoped it would do the job. The 9mm was a little light for a bear. Garen moved beside her.

"I'll take care of it." He settled the rifle butt on his shoulder and fired. When the report from the weapon had settled, he said, "The choppers are ready to load us, but first, I listened in. You weren't exactly truthful in the plane."

Miranda squared her shoulders. "No, and I'm sure you know why I couldn't tell you I shifted and killed in animal form. Can I go back inside and get my bag?"

His mouth split into a grin she could only half see in the darkness. "From now on, tell me the truth."

"You got it, sir. My bag?" she repeated.

"Yeah, you can retrieve it. Assuming my laptop's still in one piece, I need to collect it and my briefcase." He snorted back laughter. "You've been so much trouble, it's tempting to leave you behind, but don't worry, we won't."

"Gee, thanks." She recognized clandestine ops humor when she heard it. Something nagged in the back of her mind, deeper than simple, unrequited yearning for Garen. He'd appeared familiar in his animal form, but timber wolves looked a lot alike, and it had been very dark.

Sharp night vision was more the purview of cats than wolves. More importantly, his scent wasn't in her memory, which likely meant she was wrong, and their paths had never crossed. Maybe he was just a shape-shifting wolf and not lycan at all. There were a few salient differences, all of which related to magic. If that was so, hers was stronger, and he couldn't create new shifters by biting them, which probably meant he'd never been to the annual lycan gathering.

The more she thought about it, the more likely it seemed he wasn't lycan. For all the years she'd dutifully attended gatherings—particularly since Lucifer took over—she'd have run into him.

CHAPTER 8

Two weeks later

Garen ran along the asphalt track that skirted Puget Sound from Seattle's waterfront north. Sweat dripped from his forehead, and he mopped it with an equally damp arm. After the disaster outside Index, he'd put Miranda in one of the employee apartments at company headquarters. It was the only reasonable choice, but knowing she was bathing and dressing and sleeping only a few feet from where he worked had been agony. In truth, he'd gotten precious little actual work done.

About an hour ago he'd stepped into Rubicon International's downstairs gym to find her clad in a leotard that left absolutely nothing to the imagination. She was running through martial arts movements, so intent on her training regimen she hadn't known he stood just inside the glass door. Watching the fluid lines of her body as she pivoted, chopped, and leapt gave him a raging hard-on. Coming didn't make a dent in the lust setting fire to his nerves. He'd jacked off enough in the last two weeks to make himself sore. What he wanted—no, what he craved—was more of Miranda.

He'd replayed making love to her in the airplane so many times there wasn't a nanosecond of their time together he hadn't memorized. The way her mouth felt beneath his. The stiffness of her nipples in his fingers. The heat of her pussy wrapped around his shaft, fitting as though they were made for one another. Sometimes, it seemed her scent still lingered on his fingertips and in his nostrils. It drove him mad with longing.

At least during the day, he could pretend to divert himself with work. Nights were close to intolerable. He'd taken to returning to his house, rather than sleeping at the office, because he didn't trust himself not to walk into her quarters and crush her to him. Putting distance between them hadn't brought him peace of mind, though. He lay in bed and tossed and turned until he gave up and either switched to his lycan form or took a sleeping pill. The latter was safer. When he was a wolf, he wanted to run and run and run, losing his anguish in the simple beauty of movement. He lived in one of the older homes on Capitol Hill. While some wooded areas provided cover, provided he didn't leave his fenced grounds, he would've ended up running around his house. Not particularly satisfying, but if he jumped his fence, he'd run into late-night joggers—or lovers.

Garen's lungs pumped like a bellows. He could've done without thinking about lovers. He pushed himself to run harder. Passing couples with their arms wrapped around each another, staring into one another's eyes, was torture. He couldn't imagine life without Miranda. Yet he didn't see how he could bring his dreams of holding her close and whispering love words into her ear out of the shadows. It was too risky—with far too many entanglements.

I've got to think of her as an employee again. I'll drive myself mad if I can't get past this.

We could be linked through the mate bond, an insidious inner voice piped up, forcing Garen to at least consider it. Mate bonds were two way streets, though, and Miranda hadn't shown the slightest inclination toward him.

At first, he thought time would help. It hadn't. At least not the two weeks that had just passed. He grimaced. If anything, he was worse off now than he'd been the day he escorted Miranda to the well-guarded Company apartments and left her there.

At least there hadn't been any more attempts on her life. Garen had feelers out, but ISL was lying low. The one thing that had dragged him from the morass of his unrequited love hell was planning to annihilate the San Diego headquarters. Garen was surprised the dying bear had told the truth. Maybe he was sick of whatever role he played in the human trafficking organization. Counter to the U.S. government's beliefs, shifters usually had fairly decent morals. Garen would've liked to know how the bear got mixed up with ISL in the first place, might even have offered him work—if he'd discovered him in time. He had a few Company employees who'd defected from a variety of "other sides."

He passed a marker, knew he'd come five miles, and turned back. As they always did, his thoughts retuned to Miranda. What was it about her? He'd never been so besotted before. He felt like a randy teenager, smitten for the first time. If she smiled at him, his heart soared. If she walked past him, his cock hardened. He had to get a handle on his feelings before the San Diego operation. They were out of control.

Worse, when he'd asked for volunteers for San Diego, she'd been the first to step forward. It was same thing he would've done, and he was secretly proud of her, which didn't help matters. In spite of that, he was hunting for a valid reason to tell her she couldn't go. Something better than, *I do not want you putting yourself at risk.* For Christ's sake, *risk* was where they lived.

The epicenter for ISL's stateside operation was actually in San Ysidro. Garen figured it was strategically placed as close to Tijuana as it could be and still be on U.S. soil. That way, if any of the human properties got too hot to handle, they could be shipped south of the border. Garen and several of his key operatives had intuited that ISL's digs weren't in Mexico because the level of lawlessness was so extreme, it would've taken a gated compound, patrolled 24/7, to keep the goods safe.

Garen slowed his pace. He wasn't far from the office and needed to cool down—in more ways than one. Still thinking about Roulan and his artfully planned and executed ISL firm, Garen grudgingly gave the outlaw kudos. San Ysidro bought ISL the best of both worlds. It could take advantage of Mexico's chaos when it needed to and masquerade as a U.S. business the rest of the time.

Garen had ninety percent of a plan in place. They'd go in at night with plastique and blow the place to hell. That was the easy part. First, they needed to somehow ascertain how many people were being held there and free them. Garen had tried to convince himself they'd be collateral damage if there were only a few, but his conscience had rebelled, right along with Miranda.

A corner of his mouth turned downward. She'd squared her shoulders and tossed the hair she didn't have anymore back over her shoulders—an unconscious gesture it would take her years to get over, if she ever did. After that, she'd skewered him with her blue gaze and told him she wanted to go undercover.

"Let them capture me," she'd insisted. "I can organize the women and kids and break them out. It won't be that hard."

Rubicon International offices were a block away. Garen slowed to a walk. He'd nearly had a heart attack when she'd done what agents do: put her life on the line for a good cause. Of course Miranda didn't see it that way. Like all operatives volunteering for danger, she was convinced she'd come out alive. He pushed his tongue against his teeth. Part of him was angry—at himself. He'd boxed himself into a corner when he let his long-denied lust for Miranda get the better of him in the plane. Spending those few moments with her, and then the hours at the Index cabin, had only whetted his appetite for more.

More.

That was the problem. He wanted all he could get of her. Damn if he could see a ready way out. He slapped his hand on the electronic keypad next to the front door of Rubicon International's offices, let himself inside, and headed for the private elevator in the back that led to his personal suite. He had his own bathroom and shower and even a small bedroom on the top floor. On the way across the marble-inlaid lobby, he decided to stand under the shower jets until he could think again—or until he ran out of hot water. His cock pressed against the front of his running shorts, belling them out beneath their elastic waistband. Garen hustled. He draped his windbreaker over one arm and held it in front of his midsection, hoping he wouldn't run into any of his employees.

His elevator ran off a key. He fished it from his shorts, inserted it, and breathed a sigh of relief when the metal doors whooshed shut behind him.

"You're a stupid shit. You know that?"

His wolf's voice startled Garen. *"Where'd that come from?"* he demanded.

"Miranda is our mate, and you're blind to it."

"No," Garen retorted. *"You're the one who's blind. If she was our mate, she'd want us right back."*

He stepped out of the elevator into his suite of offices, waiting for a snappy rejoinder from the wolf, but one never came.

MIRANDA LIFTED her leg to the bar mounted along the wall of Rubicon International's state-of-the-art gym, and then she moved it against the wall in a vertical splits maneuver. She glanced at the clock. No wonder she was breathing hard. She'd been at it for over two hours.

"It's not like there's much else to do," she muttered and pushed into the stretch.

She'd been a virtual prisoner at Rubicon International's main offices on the Seattle waterfront since the night the choppers rescued them from the Index cabin. She'd asked Garen about letting her go home. The last time she asked, after a briefing around the upcoming San Diego/San Ysidro operation, he'd furled his brows and told her she'd be the first to know when he was tired of housing and feeding her.

Miranda changed legs. Her left one wasn't as limber, and this particular stretch nearly killed it. A familiar pain, far more pressing than the one in her ligaments and tendons, settled around her heart. She tried to ignore it, but it wouldn't leave her alone. The clean, beautiful planes of Garen's face shimmered before her. She wanted to feel his chiseled lips on hers again, trailing promise as they ran a fiery path down her neck and breasts. Her clit ached with need. Her breasts felt heavy. She'd been almost permanently aroused since right before Garen made love to her on the airplane.

Yeah, and what got me going then was thinking about him.

Miranda had tried every trick in her arsenal to focus on other things. There'd been a few two- and three-hour blocks when she managed to actually accomplish something without mooning over Garen like a lovesick kid, but those were few and far between. There were so many things she wanted to talk to him about. Like what sort of wolf shifter he was and when he'd first shifted and if he'd had supportive family around to help him.

Her first shift had come when she was fourteen. Miranda remembered the odd pressure she'd felt inside her body and the wolf images that filled her mind. One long, lazy summer evening, the possibility of actually being the wolf in her mind seemed so real she gave into it. In seconds, her T-shirt and shorts lay in shreds on the flowered carpet of her upstairs bedroom. Her senses were painfully acute, and her body felt so odd she wondered if someone had slipped drugs into her dinner. She caught a glimpse of herself in her bedroom mirror just before her aunt slammed into her room.

"Abomination," she'd screeched. "You're just like your mother. I've been waiting for this." Aunt Ellie flapped her hands at Miranda. "Find your human side again. Now. Do it now."

A revolver dangled from her aunt's hand. Fear shot adrenaline through Miranda. Her wolf looked longingly at the open window and suggested they jump through, but Miranda was too frightened to do anything but her damnedest to obey her aunt. It took several attempts before she stood, naked and panting, in the pink and white bedroom that no longer looked like hers.

Ellie's eyes were hard green stones. "I've been watching you close since you started to bleed. That was when my sister, uh…" She shook her head. "Never mind." Her aunt's face held a pinched expression. "Put some clothes on. Those—" she pointed at the floor "—aren't good for anything but the rag bin. You'll pay me back out of your babysitting money."

Miranda had grabbed a robe off the end of her bed and wrapped it around herself, her heart going like a trip hammer. "Please—" she'd held out both hands "—I need to understand."

Aunt Ellie marched right up to her then and grabbed her face between hands that felt like pincers. "The only thing you need to know, young lady, is you cannot do that and remain here—or anywhere else." She lowered her voice. "If anyone finds out, they'll kill you. I could be imprisoned if they discovered I knew about you and didn't turn you in."

Tears rolled down Miranda's face. "Who are *they*, and why do they hate me?"

"It's not you, child." Ellie's voice softened. "It's shifters. You can't be a shifter and live like a free person. I'm sorry. Maybe if you don't give in to the temptation again, it will be easier to control. Your mom used to tell me she wished she hadn't spent so much time running free as a wolf. I worried myself sick about her for years. It was almost a relief when something besides the law got her."

Ellie pulled the door shut behind her, and Miranda gathered her scraps of torn clothing. She sank into a chair, too shocked to do anything but stare at a wall. The wolf—her wolf—snarled deep inside her. It wanted to be free. Its small taste of embodiment had been heady. It wanted more.

"Holy crap." Her eyes had filled with tears on that long-ago summer evening. "What on earth am I going to do?"

Miranda dragged her thoughts back to the present. She'd moved automatically through her cool-down routine. Another few stretches and she'd be ready to shower. Her life since that first shift had been full of subterfuge, stealth, and bargains with her wolf to keep that side hidden.

No wonder I became a secret agent. My illustrious career actually began when I was a freshman in high school.

She'd found if she slipped out her window a couple nights a week and gave the wolf free rein in the fields around their house, it was controllable the rest of the time. Mostly. Her aunt pretended the night in Miranda's bedroom never happened. Miranda went along with her. It was easier that way.

She'd kept to herself during college; it didn't seem safe to get close to anyone. While she'd screwed a lycan or two at the annual gathering, she'd never had sex as a human with a human—until Garen. The experience had been so unbelievable, she dreamed about it every night, wakening with damp thighs and a pussy desperate to be full of his cock again.

She walked into the small ladies' locker room, dropped her clothes on a bench, and trooped to the shower. First too hot, then too cold, it took just the right touch to get the water so it didn't scald or freeze her. Standing beneath its spray, she erected the wall she'd always kept around her heart, brick by brick.

Garen had made it patently clear he had no interest in her—beyond their employee-employer relationship. He'd kept his distance since dumping her in the apartment right below his office. And he made a point of leaving every night. She knew because the building felt empty without his energy. No more burning the midnight oil. It was such a departure from his normal schedule where she'd gotten used to being able to catch him at work at ten p.m., or even midnight, she wondered if he might not have a girlfriend.

It doesn't matter. He was just a dream.

Walling off her feelings didn't ease the ache in her chest. She wondered if she'd ever be the same person. When she realized she was crying, Miranda pounded the tiled enclosure with a fist. "Stop it," she growled. "Just stop it. I'm bigger than this. I am not going to throw away my career—never mind my sanity—on someone who doesn't want me."

"You told him you didn't want him." Her wolf's voice came out of the blue.

"No," Miranda countered. *"What I told him was what we'd done was wrong because I work for him."*

"Amounts to the same thing," her wolf declared before subsiding into silence.

Miranda turned off the water and dried herself, waiting for the wolf to say more, but it didn't. Not surprising since the wolf rarely engaged her in conversation.

She tossed the towel in a hamper and glanced at her reflection in the steamy mirrors. Her short hair was always a surprise. Miranda had already began growing it back out. She didn't like herself as a blonde, and she missed being able to braid her hair and get it out of the way. It was too short now to do much of anything but blow in her face.

She got into fresh underwear, a pair of dark slacks, and a pressed, white shirt, following them with her workout shoes. Next, she folded her leotard and tights and headed for the stairs. The gym was in the basement. She always took the stairs to and from her workouts. For one thing, they ate up more time than the elevator.

I've got to get out of here. I don't have enough to do.

Miranda let herself into the neutrally furnished room she'd occupied for the past thirteen days. It had a stellar view of Puget Sound. She checked her computer, responded to a few emails, and went to work on logistics for the ISL takedown operation. She'd floated the idea of setting herself up inside the San Ysidro facility after scoping it out via the sat feed. Garen hadn't exactly said no, so she buried herself in research and began making lists of what she'd need to go undercover.

For once, time passed quickly. She was surprised to look up and notice night had fallen. She glanced at the clock. Eight. Time to find something to eat. Rubicon International's cafeteria was lined with vending machines, but she was sick to death of them.

Miranda looked longingly out the window at a little Thai place across the street. How long would it take to order something, run over there, and pick it up? Their phone number flashed in red neon. She picked up her cell phone to call and blew out a breath. Garen had been painstakingly clear. She needed to get permission to leave the premises. If she needed anything—anything at all—she was to find one of the other agents and send them to get it.

Anger flared. Goddammit. Her boss was treating her like a ten-year-old. Riding high on indignation, she punched a different number into her phone: his.

He picked up on the second ring. "Yes, Miranda." A husky undertone in his voice suggested he'd been fucking someone.

Fine, she thought sourly. *So what if he has? I don't own him.*

Not even close, sweetheart, her sarcastic inner maven chimed.

Miranda shut her eyes. Pain washed through her. Christ, but she hoped she'd get over him—and damned soon. It hurt so godawful much, she nearly couldn't stand it.

"What do you need?" A note of impatience crept into Garen's voice.

"I, um, you see—"

"Spit it out, Miss Miller."

"I want to order takeout Thai food from across the street." Heat rose from her open collar and suffused her face. She sounded like a total dumbass. "Look. It was a bad idea. I'm sorry I—"

"I have a better idea," he cut in smoothly. "I'm actually still upstairs. How about if I come down and take you out to dinner. We can kill two birds with one stone since there are some things I want to discuss with you."

Guess I was wrong about him being lip-locked with another woman.

Her mouth gaped open and closed. She sucked air. Had he just asked her on a date?

I'm pathetic. He asked me to join him for the equivalent of a business lunch.

A sigh rattled against her ear. "Look. If you'd rather, I can run and get you Thai takeout. That way you won't have to eat with me."

"No. I, uh, um, I'd enjoy having company. It's been pretty lonely since I've been here."

No lonelier than when I'm at home, but he doesn't have to know that.

"It's settled, then. Shall we say fifteen minutes?"

"Sure."

She glanced at the display. He'd disconnected. Miranda sprinted for the bathroom and brushed her teeth, and then her hair. Her locks were thick and refused to do anything but hang in loose curls. She looped them behind her ears, peered critically at her face in the mirror, and opened the drawer that held her spartan makeup bag. She glanced at the pots of color and settled for the thinnest gloss of gold eye shadow and a pale lip tint. It would never do for him to notice she'd put on makeup for him.

"It is not a date," she told the mirror firmly.

Yes, but it might be an opportunity.

Returning to the bedroom, she stripped off her plain, practical shirt, donned a lacy plunge bra, and slipped a formfitting, pale green jersey over it. The black slacks and tennis shoes were fine.

Before she could stop herself, she'd spritzed Spanish Amber perfume behind both ears and in the hollow between her collarbones. Mouth dry, nipples hard, clit swollen, she wondered if she'd be able to eat a thing. She'd just stuffed her phone into a small purse when Garen knocked at her door.

CHAPTER 9

Garen's nostrils twitched. He'd smelled Miranda's wonderful scents the minute he walked out the stairwell door and into the corridor where her apartment was located. Rich and sensual, they hit him in the groin. He hadn't thought he could get any harder; he'd been wrong. He wore a ridiculously oversized dark sweatshirt. It covered his shoulder holster and his erection. His face felt flushed. The sweatshirt wouldn't hide that.

For a fleeting moment, he considered bolting back into the stairwell to compose himself, and then he set his jaw in a determined line. It wouldn't matter what he did. The reality of Miranda right next to him would undo any equanimity he managed to latch onto. He raised his fist and tapped on her door.

It opened so quickly, he was certain she'd been poised right on the other side. The second he saw her, his eyes widened. She'd donned a clingy, moss-green top that molded to her high, firm breasts. Her nipples were visible poking against the fabric. Her newly blonde-streaked hair just brushed her shoulders and set off her blue eyes. He'd never truly appreciated the exotic cant to her cheekbones before. They gave her a cat-like look. He inhaled and realized she'd put on perfume—for him. Lust flamed so hot he was surprised it didn't burn him to a cinder where he stood.

She took a step toward him. "Are we ready to go, or are you just going to stand there staring at me?" A husky undertone made her voice sound like liquid honey.

Between her breasts and her voice and the reality of having her inches from him, Garen's carefully scripted, *Sure. I made us reservations at La Traviata*, frittered away like so much dust. He closed the distance between them, wrapped his arms around her, and slashed his mouth down over hers. Half of him expected her to judo chop him, but her mouth opened under his, and she wound her arms around his shoulders, pressing her breasts into his chest. Where it was sandwiched between them, his cock jumped against her belly.

He kicked the door shut. She straddled one of his legs between hers and ground herself against him. Her breath came fast against his mouth that was glued to hers. She made a feral sound and dropped her hands to his ass so she could pull his body tighter against her. He broke the kiss and leaned back to look at her. Eyes shut, cheeks flushed, mouth swollen from their kiss, she was the most beautiful woman he'd ever laid eyes on.

His throat was so thick, it was hard to talk. "Last time you said it was a mistake. I need to hear you say you want me before I lose every last bit of control and rip your clothes off."

Her incredible eyes opened, and she met his gaze. "It was a mistake. This will be too, but I'll be damned if I care." She let go of him, took a step backward, and pulled her top over her head. Her amazing breasts spilled over the top of a cream lace bra. She bent to unlace her shoes and toed them off, and then undid her slacks. They slid down her legs and pooled around her feet. She stepped out of them. Black curls peeked from around the edges of a matching thong panty. The crotch was dark with her juices.

Garen couldn't tear his gaze away. He hadn't seen her body when they'd grappled with one another in the Learjet. It was perfect. Generous breasts rode high on a shapely ribcage. Her shoulders were muscular, yet feminine at the same time. A flat stomach, flared hipbones, and long, well-formed legs took his breath away. Tongue-tied and awkward, he knew he was staring but couldn't help himself.

"Well?" She placed her hands on those wonderful naked hips and quirked a brow. "You may be worth waiting for, but you did promise me dinner. I'll hold you to it—afterward."

He heard the growl form deep in his throat. In seconds, his sweatshirt, shoulder holster, and gun lay in a heap on the floor. He stepped out of his loafers and reached for the waistband of his pants, but she beat him to it. She followed his pants down and knelt before him. His cock shuddered with anticipation.

Miranda licked all around his glans, little teasing licks and nibbles that drove him mad. He wouldn't last. Not this time, but he'd get hard again. Around Miranda, he was always hard. She took his shaft into her mouth and worked him with both hands. He captured her head to show her the rhythm he needed. Her teeth scraped delicate flesh. Not too hard, just enough to ratchet his pleasure up another few notches. She tightened her grip.

Garen's balls snugged against his body. He'd never experienced anything as intense as her mouth and hands urging him onward. There was heat and hunger in her movements, as if she'd imagined sucking him off in her dreams. Who knew, maybe she fantasized about him just as much as he did about her.

Not possible...

And then he stopped thinking. The wonderful sensations began in the pit of his stomach and swirled out in burning, juddering bursts. She sucked harder, draining him.

He tugged himself out of her mouth and slid to the floor next to her. He covered her passion-swollen mouth with his, tasting himself on her, and pushed her onto her back. After stopping for a long moment to admire her, he strung kisses down her neck, and she arched into his touch. He pushed her bra aside and took a breast into his mouth, suckling and laving the nipple. Already hard, it stiffened more under his touch. He dipped a hand between her legs, easily bypassing the slender nylon thong. She was drenched. The musk of her arousal made him crazy with need. Never mind he'd just come.

He slithered farther down her body and took her panties off so he could settle his mouth over her swollen nub. She bucked against him and buried her hands in his hair. Her clit stiffened still more under his ministrations. She drove herself rhythmically against his mouth, crying and moaning. He slid fingers inside her pussy and felt the contractions of her orgasm squeeze him. He sucked harder, wanting to extend her pleasure.

Once her body quieted, he knelt over her and took her hips between his hands. "Turn over."

She opened eyes misted by heat-lust and looked at him. "We're good to go," she said breathlessly. "You came, I came—"

"We're not done, Miranda. Either I'll fuck you this way, or you can get on your hands and knees." Desire, feral and savage, knifed through him. This woman was *his*. All his. Whether she knew it or not. No matter how many times he took her, it would never be enough.

With an inborn athleticism, she flipped over. The perfect globes of her perfect ass parted, displaying wet folds framed by dark curls. The rational part of him vanished. With a fierce cry he barely recognized as his voice, he wrapped a hand around his cock and drove it home inside her. He pulled nearly all the way out, swirled the tip of him around her opening, and jammed himself in to the hilt. After a dozen long, slow strokes, both of them lost it. She pressed back against him over and over.

He hung onto a ragged edge of control. She would come again, goddammit, before he did. She was close. He felt it in the tension of her muscles and saw it in the corded lines of her throat. She screamed, and her pussy muscles clenched around him. He snaked a hand to her clit, making absolutely certain she was as high as she could get. Somewhere in the midst of all that, he released inside her. Garen came hard, and he just kept coming.

They ended up in a panting, sweaty heap on the carpeted floor. "Now do I finally get dinner?" She moved out from beneath him. "After I rinse off, that is."

Miranda got to her feet in a single lithe movement. He watched her walk to the bathroom, her body a study in female perfection.

"Here." A wet washcloth hurled through the air at him.

He laughed and caught it. "I can take a hint." He got to his feet and joined her at the sink.

"It's handy you're a sh—um, like me. No worries about pregnancy or diseases."

"You're right to be cautious about what you say," he murmured, "but I'm the only one who listens to the audio feed from the rooms here."

She resettled her breasts in her bra and went to gather the rest of her clothes, trading her soaked thong for a clean one. He dressed too. Miranda looked as if she wanted to say something, so he gave her space. Bag over her shoulder, she walked to the door and turned to face him.

"I don't know what this thing between us is, but maybe what we just did will lay it to rest." She dropped her gaze, inhaled sharply, and then looked at him again. "I can't work for you and fuck you. It's just wrong. Never mind Rubicon's policies. But I can't stop thinking about you, either."

"Miranda—" He started to tell her he loved her, that they were mates and they'd figure something out, but she shook her head.

"No, hear me out. What happened in the airplane was sort of like an appetizer. Maybe actually getting naked together and sating ourselves will mean I can reclaim myself."

He swallowed. "Do you feel like you've had enough of me?"

Her cheeks turned crimson. "No, but we're standing in a room that reeks of lust and sex."

He tossed his head back and laughed. "You win, Miss Miller. Lead out, and we'll scare up a late dinner."

"Where are we going?"

"I'd made us reservations at La Traviata. It won't matter we're not on time. I booked a private room for the evening." Garen followed her out the door.

Maybe it's better to think like she does, he told himself. *I have no fucking idea how to address either the office romance or potentially having my Lucifer identity outed.*

He'd been surprised she never followed up on their conversation from the forest outside the Index cabin. Maybe she decided she'd been mistaken about him looking familiar and was letting the whole thing drop. He hoped so.

MIRANDA TOOK another mouthful from the selection of delectable pastas on her plate. Dinner had gone well until she'd reiterated her plan to infiltrate ISL's San Ysidro facility. Garen had made it quite clear he didn't want her involved. She picked her next words with care and pitched her voice low.

"This is one of the reasons why what we did earlier was a bad idea. You've gotten all protective of me. I can't have you treating me any different from the other agents. For one thing, they'll notice."

"And you think they haven't noticed us studiously avoiding one another since we got back from the East Coast?"

She shrugged. "Maybe. Look. I need to work. I'm far from independently wealthy. I could go back into the Army—at least for a little while longer. Thirty-five used to be the cut-off age for new Berets, and I'd likely have to start all over."

"Is that what you want?" He reached across the table for her hand, but she moved it away.

She shook her head. "Better if you don't touch me. I like working for Rubicon International, but if you and I can't get back to something normal, I'll have to leave. If you were honest with yourself, you'd understand that too."

I feel conflicted as hell about all of this, but I'm not going to tell him that.

"Fine." He narrowed his blue eyes. "One of the things about working for me is you take orders—"

"Which is one more reason we can't be lovers. There's got to be some equality in love relationships. How well do you think it would work if you pulled rank—like you're doing now—and forced my compliance on something?"

His mouth twitched. "Obviously, not well at all. There are lots of good reasons why your San Ysidro idea isn't sound. You're just not listening to them."

"I'm the strongest woman agent on the payroll. I'm attractive. I know I can inveigle my way inside. None of the other women who work for Rubicon International would have as good a chance."

"It's too risky."

"Me going to Amsterdam alone was risky, but you didn't tell me *no* then. The only thing that's changed is you got your dick inside me." Miranda dropped her fork onto her plate. Her hand balled into a fist. Anger made her jaw tight. Worse, tears weren't far beneath the surface.

"You're not being fair."

She rolled her eyes. "Yeah, Garen. Life isn't fair, but we pick our path and make our choices. You cannot protect me from the bad guys. You'll hate what I turn into if you shove me behind your shadow and force me to take cover."

His face developed a closed-off look she recognized. She looked away and concentrated on what was left of her dinner despite not being hungry anymore.

Damn it. I knew better. Why, oh why, did I let my body have the upper hand?

An image of them making love played in her mind. He was the best, the most perfect man imaginable. Not only was his body a work of art, he knew instinctively how to touch her in all her special places. Even better, he was a shifter, so she wouldn't have to worry about keeping that part of herself hidden from him.

"Penny for your thoughts, Miss Miller."

She started, ripped from her musings. "Uh, nothing special. Why?"

He shrugged. "You've been scraping your fork back and forth over an empty plate, and you have a faraway look in your eyes. If you're still hungry, I can ask them to bring more."

He sounded so kind, it nearly undid her. "No. I'm fine. Maybe some dessert, and then I need to get back to my room." She pressed her lips together.

"What?"

"I want to go home. It's been two weeks. If ISL was planning to send another assault force after me, they'd have done it by now."

"You don't know that."

"Damn it! You just want to keep me under lock and key. I'm not in the Witness Protection Program. Even if I were, I'd have more freedom than I do right now. Remember what I said about choices?" He nodded. "Well, I made mine when I chose a career in espionage. I accepted risk, danger, and maybe even death. Don't try to make me into something I'm not. Please."

To her horror, a tear tracked down one cheek. She ignored it. Maybe he wouldn't notice.

"Holy shit. Are you crying?" He scooted his chair next to hers and closed his arms awkwardly around her from the side.

"No. I'm fine. Please don't touch me anymore. I can't be me when you're that close. I can't think. I can't—" Her voice broke, and she wrenched her body out of his grasp. Getting to her feet, she moved her chair to the opposite side of the table. "I'm going to find the ladies' room. I changed my mind about dessert. Once I get back, I want to leave."

Miranda pushed blindly through the door of their private dining room. She looked up and down the hallway and located a bathroom. Once inside, she locked herself in a stall and sank onto the commode's closed lid. Tears sat hot and bitter just behind her eyes. She forced them to stay there.

What the fuck is wrong with me? I'm a maudlin mess. If this is what sex turns me into, I don't need it.

It's not just sex, a wiser, older, inner voice said. *I'm falling in love. I was mostly there before he ever laid a hand on me.*

"*He's our mate,*" her wolf spoke up.

"*Bullshit. There's no such thing. Shifter mates are urban legend.*"

"*If you were one of the older ones, you'd know—*"

The outer door opened. Miranda girded herself, but at least her wolf shut up.

If Garen had followed her, she didn't quite know what she'd do. She peeked beneath the stall door and was incredibly grateful to see a dark blue pair of high heels. Since she was in the only stall, she took a few deep breaths, flushed to make her being in the stall a bit more realistic, and let herself into the small bathroom.

A tall, leggy redhead with green eyes glanced at her, looked away, and then said, "It's none of my business, honey, but you're looking like you just lost your best friend. Man problems?"

"You don't know the half of it." Miranda ginned up half a smile and rinsed her hands at the sink.

"You won't take my advice, but I'm gonna give it to you anyway," the redhead went on. "Never let 'em know they got under your skin. It's better that way. Lets you keep the upper hand. You know?"

"Uh, thanks."

"Don't mention it. Sorry." The woman ducked into the stall. "I'd love to stand here and chat, but I've gotta go. My eyes are floating."

Miranda left the bathroom. Garen stood outside the door to their dining room, obviously waiting for her. "You've overseen one too many clandestine operations," she whispered when she got close. "I only went to the john."

"Can't be too careful. Here." He handed her purse and jacket over. "You said you wanted to leave."

She took her things and walked toward the exit, grateful that for once he'd taken her request seriously. "Thanks."

"I thought about some of the things you said—" He held the outer door of the restaurant open for her.

"And?" She turned to face him once they were outside.

"If you really want to go home, you can go tomorrow."

She tried to read his face, but it was closed to her. "Why not tonight?"

"I want to spend what's left of it trolling through my computer networks to make certain I didn't just make a bad call."

The valet brought their car around. Garen held the door for her and went around to the driver's side. They rode in silence for a few minutes. When he spoke again, the words sounded tortured. "I value you as an employee, Miranda. I'm not going to do anything else that might jeopardize that. Someday you'll make some man very happy. I wish it were me, but you're correct, we can't be lovers and work together. I'm not going to fire you, so I promise to keep my feelings under better control."

Feelings? What feelings?

Did he have feelings beyond pure lust for her? She opened her mouth to ask and shut it. Safer not to go there. It was a lose-lose proposition. If he said no, she'd be hurt since she was falling in love with him. If he said yes, she'd be devastated by the might-have-beens.

"One more thing, Miss Miller." His voice was raspy, broken, as if he'd just lost something precious.

Her heart ached—for both of them. She nodded, and then realized he was watching the road. "What?"

"We're having a final strategy session at fifteen hundred tomorrow for San Ysidro. You're welcome to come and pitch your case. The final decision is up to the team."

"Thank you, sir." It was so much more than she'd expected that a confusing welter of feelings pummeled her. "Why'd you change your mind?"

"I don't want to make you hide in my shadow, or however you put it earlier. Now, if you wouldn't mind, I'd just as soon end this conversation."

CHAPTER 10

Garen paced up and down his opulent office at Rubicon International's headquarters. Carved wainscoting ran up the walls, depicting medieval scenes featuring famous spies. Thick, imported Oriental rugs cushioned his steps. Usually the combination of rich wood, Eastern art, and huge windows that looked out on Seattle's waterfront quieted his nerves, but not today.

The San Ysidro team had been distressingly enthusiastic about Miranda's plan to go undercover as a call girl. She was certain she could entice ISL's operatives to scoop her into the cadre of women they sold on the open market. Between her short hair and colored contacts to turn her eyes brown, she'd exuded confidence no one would recognize her.

"Shit," he muttered. "She's probably right. It's unlikely anyone who saw her in Amsterdam would be in San Ysidro." Regardless, he couldn't send her off without fully vetting her as an RI agent. Not now, when she'd become the center of his universe.

Tenured status would give her the right to know all the rest of them were shifters too. She'd have the best equipment and be bound to Rubicon International by her blood, which would give Garen—and the other tenured operatives—access to her mind. The blood bond would also allow her to communicate with the rest of the team telepathically over distances—a critical element if someone in San Ysidro recognized her.

He shook his head. He didn't particularly want to see inside her mind. He loved her. Forcing himself to stand by the words he'd spoken driving back from the restaurant two nights before was tearing his heart into bitter, pointed shards.

He glanced at a grandfather clock. In just a few minutes, he'd escort Miranda to her final test. They'd conferred privately after the San Ysidro team meeting, and he'd made noises about dispensing with the last hurdle standing between her and full standing as an agent at Rubicon International. She'd been horrified by the prospect of him bending even so much as one rule on her behalf. He'd been proud of her.

Rubicon International vetted its operatives through a number of increasingly difficult assignments. Only about half the recruits made it through. Most firms that provided murder-for-hire personnel engaged criminals or sociopaths. Garen couldn't stand to be around them. Their energy made his skin crawl. He preferred his method: find people with aptitude, train them right, and hope for the best. Assassination was an art. Just like any trade, it could be taught, and Rubicon International had an excellent track record.

His teeth gritted against one another. Garen made an effort to relax his jaws. He wanted to shift. His wolf always calmed him, but there wasn't time. He felt claws close to the surface. They pressed against the ends of his fingertips and toes. One emerged from a finger, black and gleaming. He stared at it in disbelief. Could his control be getting away from him?

Surely I'm not that upset.

He stomped to a corner of the room where a gouge in the wood wouldn't be as noticeable and growled before running his claw down the groove between the walls so hard it practically left sparks. Because he couldn't help himself, he did it again. A fine mist of wood chips fell to the carpet. He shoved them deep into the corner with the tip of one impeccably polished loafer.

"Damn it."

The claw retracted, and he slammed a fist into the wood. He'd broken one of his own cardinal rules. Never get emotionally involved with the help. What if things went badly today and Miranda was killed? What then?

What if things turn to shit in San Ysidro? No matter how this ends up, I've fucked myself. I'll never be able to send her out on an assignment again and not either follow her or worry myself sick the entire time she's gone.

He bashed the wall again with his fist. Pain had a steadying effect. For the briefest of moments, he thought about calling the whole thing off. He'd just tell Miranda she had tenure regardless of her feelings about being treated like any other agent and fulfilling each and every requirement.

He wasn't certain what he'd do about today's other agent, Ted Adamson, waiting in the field for Miranda. Garen slammed his forehead against the palm of one hand. Ted was Miranda's test, but part of her task was figuring that out.

He wasn't certain about Ted. The man claimed to be a shifter—and he'd passed all his tests—but Garen had his doubts. Ted always came up with one excuse or another when it was time to shift. Even with the blood bond, Garen had trouble truly seeing behind the man's carefully constructed defenses. No, if Garen called off Miranda's test, he'd have to do something drastic, or the other agent would tell everyone Miranda didn't deserve to be part of Rubicon International, that the boss pulled the plug on her final assignment.

"What the fuck?" He reproached himself. "Am I really going to put the whole company at risk just because she has the hottest little ass I've seen in a couple hundred years, and I'd kill to fuck her again?"

Call a spade a spade, his inner voice answered. *I'm focusing on sex because acknowledging how much I care about her rips me to shreds.*

His cock swelled. So hard it was almost painful, it pressed against the front panel of his suit trousers. He rubbed it, and it jerked against his hand. His gaze strayed to the clock. Reality intruded. He needed to leave now. No time to bring himself off while he fantasized about Miranda's blonde-streaked hair, saucy blue eyes, and acres of curves. Never mind her long, shapely legs and six-foot frame.

"Think about something else, goddammit," he muttered. "I can't go out there with the front of my pants belled out like a balloon."

He sucked a deep breath, followed it with another, and forced his thoughts to Rubicon International. He cared about it like the children he'd never had.

Maybe if I followed my heart, I could have some real children.

Oh, shut up.

He rolled his eyes, shrugged into his suit coat, and did the best he could to hide his erection. Miranda would be waiting. No matter how ambivalent he was, he had to let this gambit play itself out. His wolf side howled in protest. He wanted Miranda up front and personal, running by his side in a wooded glade. Usually his wolf was right on, but he'd made the mistake of screwing a vampire once, egged on by his randy wolf, who'd fallen hard for her lush red curls. That was the closest he'd ever come to dying. Well, not dying exactly, but he had no desire to join the ranks of the undead with their taste for human blood.

"Back off," he told the wolf. *"I want her too, but the time's not right. No more mate bond talk. She has to decide to come to us."*

And I have to decide just how much of my dual life I'm willing to disclose.

Miranda flicked a spot of lint off the hem of her black suit and fidgeted in a straight-backed chair. Her eyes darted longingly at the more comfortable chairs scattered about the plush office, but they weren't a match for her mood. Exactly where she'd placed herself had a better shot at neutralizing *edgy* and *tense* than an overstuffed chair.

A corner of her mouth twitched into a frown. Today would decide…everything. She was about to find out what would happen next in her life. For the briefest of moments, she opened her mouth, panting in nervous anticipation. Then she pulled her tongue back in and got a grip on the lycan side of her nature. Outside of Garen, no one at Rubicon International knew her secret, and she aimed to keep it that way.

A shudder coursed through her. Depending on today's outcome, either she'd be elevated to the inner circle running Rubicon International—and be allowed to carry out her San Ysidro plan, or… Or what? What happened to the ones who failed? Were they disposed of in some neat but nameless way? The way she'd dispatched others on company orders.

Garen never told her exactly how to carry out her assignments, only that someone had become extraneous. That was the word he used. Extraneous. Would some agent she'd never seen before lie in wait to do her in if she botched today's assignment? A thin string of saliva materialized out of nowhere. She balled her hands into tight fists. Her wolf was so close to the surface, it was disturbing. She hastily wiped her chin, taking care not to smear her lipstick.

Miranda exhaled raggedly, not sure which was more important: her job or Garen.

Oh, please, her inner voice snarked. *Let's get real here.*

With her heart a lead weight in her chest, she understood in a gut-wrenching flash of realization that Garen meant everything. If something went horribly wrong today and he booted her out of Company ranks, she'd never see him again.

Can't have that. Failure is not an option.

A familiar sensation nagged near the small of her back. Her tail was trying its damndest to swish back and forth. Because sitting wasn't working, she rose to her feet and swiveled her head to relax the metal bar of tension that had settled between her shoulder blades. Most of the time her human form was comfortable, but not today. Stress sometimes had that effect, though. It brought her closer to the primal parts of herself, the parts that could morph into fur and claws at a moment's notice.

Her lips curved into a predatory smile until she caught a glimpse of herself in an ornate mirror. The lupine cast to her features was disturbing enough, she took a couple of uneven breaths and forced the more rounded planes of her Miranda face back into place. Patting her cheekbones to try to ensure her face *stayed* that way, she wondered again just what Garen had in mind for her today. In her secret places, she couldn't believe he'd be the author of her destruction if she turned in a less-than-stellar performance.

No, he'll just tell me to clear out my desk and have a nice life. What kind of life can I have without him, though?

She caught the sound of distant footsteps. Miranda recognized the pattern and cadence of those steps and folded back into her seat. Garen was coming. Because being around him was excruciating—particularly after their last bout of sex—she'd adopted her Army persona and was doing her damndest to be a good soldier and follow orders. Besides, if she stayed on her feet, there was a chance she'd throw herself into his arms and latch her mouth onto his. Seconds later the door opened with a metallic, whooshing sound as the electronics activated.

"Right on time as always, Miss Miller." Garen cut an impressive figure as he fixed his steely gaze on her. He was impeccably dressed in his usual dark suit, white shirt, and blue tie. The planes of his face were finely chiseled, but today he looked tired. Lines creased his forehead, and day-old stubble peppered his cheeks. She wanted to gather him into her arms and smooth away the worry lines with kisses.

I've got to bury that part of myself and damned fast.

The worst part was she thought she saw longing akin to her own in the depths of his blue eyes.

"Yes, sir." Miranda rose gracefully to her feet, prepared to receive her orders.

Instead of handing her a sheaf of destroy-these-once-you've-read-them instructions, he turned and headed for the outer doors to the building. Looking back over one shoulder, he quirked an eyebrow. "Coming?" he inquired.

Momentarily nonplussed, she started after him, and then returned for her forgotten briefcase. As she moved, her shoulder harness dug into her, and the cold metal of the gun she carried scraped against her skin. She felt fur sprout as a protection and shook herself to stop the transformation.

"Not now. Not needed."

By the time she caught up with him, Garen stood on the sidewalk in front of the vintage waterfront building that housed Rubicon International. A white Lexus SUV, one of a fleet of company cars, stood at the curb. He held the door open and gestured eloquently. She didn't need words to understand he expected her to get inside. She swallowed, her throat suddenly dry. Garen's actions were so out of character she had no idea what would come next. Normally, he gave her written instructions, added a few verbal ones on top of them, and sent her on her way.

What the fuck? I didn't prepare for this.

A different inner voice snorted. *Yeah, preparation's my middle name. Not much to do but get in the car.*

A brisk wind blew strands of hair into her face. She peeked inside the car. No driver. The implication hit her, and she had to force herself to pretend nothing was wrong. Garen obviously planned to take her somewhere, and it was just the two of them. Had he forgotten his promise to treat her like any other agent?

"Miranda." Garen looked oddly at her. "For chrissake, get in the car. I don't have all day."

She hesitated. "Where are we going? Usually, you give me—"

"I'll discuss your assignment once we're moving."

Her wolf didn't like any of this. Garen sounded cold, distant.

Only his eyes looked familiar, and they were glazed with pain. Her wolf urged her to take off running. She shushed it.

"Are you going to get in?" Irritation and something else she couldn't quite name underscored his words.

"Of course. Sorry." Miranda shot him a sunny smile and slid into the passenger seat, taking care to flash as much thigh as she could manage. Maybe, if he was ambivalent about dragging her off to a private rendezvous before her final assignment, she could up the ante a bit.

What the hell am I doing? Every time I fuck him, all I do is want him more. What am I, a masochist?

Yeah, a regular glutton for punishment, she thought glumly.

Garen laughed and ran an index finger up her exposed thigh. "That's the spirit, Miss Miller." Shoving her door shut, he came around to the driver's side and got in.

CHAPTER 11

*T*hey traveled for a while in silence. Miranda noted they were heading north on the expressway that would take them across the border into Canada. She hoped they weren't going that far. Between wrestling with her attraction for Garen and being hyped up about whatever her final assignment might be, she wanted to spring into action and get the show on the road.

Garen hummed a tuneless song that got on her nerves. Lust rolled off him in waves. She did her best to ignore the frank sexual vibrations, but it wasn't easy. The musk of his arousal filled the car and ignited her senses. Miranda had her hands full managing her wolf side, keeping her fight-or-flight energy in check, and surreptitiously rubbing her thighs together. She couldn't wait for the car ride to end. If it lasted too long, she'd jump his bones and be done with it.

"Where are we going?" she asked at last.

"Somewhere quite special." Half turning, he bared his teeth at her in what was supposed to be a smile.

Guess he's not going to tell me.

She tried to think what else she could ask that might yield a clue or two, but came up dry. The silence made her nervous and amped up her lust. Miranda reached under her jacket to readjust the Beretta digging into her ribs.

"You seem antsy, Miss Miller."

She shrugged. "I want to get this over with so I can concentrate on San Ysidro."

"You'll be paired with Ted today. He'll meet you near the target. It's up to the two of you to work together to bring down your objective."

Red flags flared in her mind. "But we always work alone," she protested, adding, "I need information about the target." She bit her lower lip.

"Correction, Miss Miller. We *usually* work alone. Ted has all the information you'll need."

"I don't like this."

"Understood. The reason you don't like it revolves about control. You're uncomfortable because you don't know more."

She snorted. "No kidding. I've never worked with Ted before. It would've been better if—"

"Uh-uh." Garen glanced sidelong at her. "I gave you a choice. You insisted on being treated like everyone else. Just because you're used to working a certain way, doesn't mean you always get to choose. Flexibility is key to being successful in the field. Consider today a test of your ability to think on your feet and work with unknown quantities."

He took an exit that led them into wooded countryside typical of the Pacific Northwest. The day was overcast, and she glanced at the digital clock on the console. Four o'clock. Days were short late in the fall, so it would be dark in less than an hour. She hoped she'd be done with whatever Garen had in mind before the sun came up. A single night without sleep was tolerable. More than that and her mind became dull and sluggish.

Doesn't take long to kill someone, she reminded herself. *That's what I'm out here for.*

"We're close to your meeting place." Garen pulled off onto a dirt road and seemed to be hunting for something, as he slowed down several times.

"What are your expectations of me?" she asked formally.

"That is your last test," he said. "There are no expectations. Your performance today will determine your future."

You mean if I even have a future with Rubicon International, she finished for him, taking care to remain silent.

The car lurched to a halt. "We're here," he announced. She waited for him to come around to open her door, when he said, "Goddammit, Miranda. Be careful."

She swiveled to face him. The corners of his eyes were pinched with concern. She reached to stroke the side of his face, knowing touching him was a mistake. "You promised not to do this."

He laid a hand over hers, capturing it next to his jaw. "You're not making it any easier."

"No, I suppose not." She bent across the console and brushed her lips across his.

He wound his arms around her and deepened the kiss, releasing her abruptly. The harsh sound of their mingled breathing filled the small space.

"Neither of us can dance on two floors," he said gruffly. "Get out. I hope to God I'll see you after this is over."

"Aren't you coming, at least until I meet up with Ted?" Alarm sluiced through her. She pushed her door open, grabbed her very unnecessary briefcase, and stood.

"No. Close the door."

The minute she did, he jammed the car into reverse, fishtailing it until he was headed back the way they'd come. Dust and gravel splattered her. She sneezed and then brushed off her clothes.

"What the fuck?"

Miranda stared after the taillights of the Lexus. Her lips still burned from their kiss. "He's just going to dump me out here. Christ! Ted's not even here yet." She shifted from foot to foot, wishing she weren't wearing high heels. A message from the animal side of her brain made her glance sharply around and take stock of her situation. Death caught the unwary. She wasn't planning on it catching her. Not today, anyway. It would be better to wait for Ted within the shadowed forest. She hadn't said anything to Garen, but what little she knew about the other agent gave her the creeps.

The deeply rutted road was lined with stately evergreens. Feeling exposed, she faded into their dimness and continued to evaluate what she had to work with. Her unseen tail swished from side to side. Light waned from the day. Could she risk shape-shifting? One of the rules Lucifer had established was they shifted at night—and only at night.

While she considered that, the sound of a car engine filled her ears. Since Garen's car had been the only one on the deserted road, and she hadn't seen any houses, she assumed this new car was probably Ted.

Miranda dropped back fifty more paces where the tree cover was even thicker. Head cocked to one side, she listened intently. The car's engine was still running, but the vehicle had come to a stop. Shrugging, she kicked off her shoes. Her feet would be cold, but she could live with that. The rattle of automatic weapon fire jarred her. She dropped to her belly, flattening herself against the dank ground.

Christ, did Rubicon International send assassins to finish me off? Is my task to kill them?

Stop! Garen wouldn't do that to me.

Deciding this qualified as the sort of emergency she could justify to Lucifer, Miranda dropped the guard she always kept over her wolf side. Usually, she stripped her clothes off first but didn't think she could spare the time. She felt her spine lengthen and her limbs move under it. Thick, gray fur with black markings took the place of her skin and hair. Within less than a minute, her tailored suit lay in tatters on the damp earth.

She pushed her gun out of the way with a paw. She'd forgotten to engage the safety, but there wasn't much she could do about it now. She growled low in the back of her throat. It was the wolf equivalent of laughter. As far as the wolf was concerned, the gun was nothing but a silly prop. She had teeth and claws and speed. Who needed guns when you had all those things?

Miranda stepped away from her torn clothing. Her lips skinned back, baring her fangs. She loved her wolf form. She'd spend more time in it if she could. She scanned the woods, her senses on full alert. Above the smells of metal and gasoline and cordite, she smelled a man. Ted? Whoever it was hadn't quit discharging automatic weapon rounds. Did that mean his assignment was to kill her? What about the mysterious target Garen had mentioned? Did it even exist?

No wonder he left so fast. Fucking pussy.

Anger vied with outrage. Sadness wasn't far behind. Had she truly meant so little to him?

Another spate of machine-gun fire split the air. She clamped her jaws together. Keeping down, belly almost scraping the ground, Miranda circled around. She wanted to see if it was Ted shooting and what his position was. For all she knew, their target had come on foot and beat Ted to the draw. Except she only smelled one man, not two or more.

Miranda rethought her strategy and went for speed. It didn't matter who was shooting. The only thing that mattered was they wanted her dead. She was certain whoever was after her wouldn't be expecting a wolf, so she streaked across the road sixty yards ahead of a Mercedes roadster and lost herself in the forest on the other side. Because the driver was facing the other way, firing out the window, so it was likely he never even noticed her.

Panting, she dug her claws into soft dirt and came to a stop. She'd recognized the car. It belonged to Ted. Unless someone had killed him and stolen his car, he was the one shooting at her. Sick outrage pounded through her.

At least this explains why Garen made up that cock-and-bull story about pairing me with Ted.

None of them ever actually worked *together*. Murder was always an individual assignment. She'd assumed it was to protect Rubicon International in case something went terribly wrong. That way there were no potential witnesses.

Was this what happened to agents she never saw again? Their co-workers were sent to annihilate them? If an operative somehow managed to beat his death sentence, did he move up the corporate ladder? Or would Garen keep sending people after her until one of them was successful? No matter how hard she tried, she couldn't get her mind around Garen wanting her dead. She resurrected the desperation of his lips on hers in the car. Men on the verge of killing someone didn't kiss like that.

Miranda tried to think. That was the only downside to her wolf form. Her ability to reason wasn't as strong as when she was human. Rubicon International had sent her on many missions, but never against another employee. At least not that she knew about. She supposed it was possible—especially since Rubicon International had many branch offices—that she'd been deployed to kill one of their own a time or two and just not known about it.

Hell, maybe every single one I killed worked for us. Except Roulan and his thugs.

That thought disturbed her, so she pushed it aside. The implication of an entire business dedicated to killing off its own workers was so bizarre, she couldn't fathom it.

She ran deeper into the trees, unsure what to do. If Ted would just get out of that damned car, she could jump him. She'd been listening and hadn't heard his car door either open or close.

Lucifer's voice pounded in her head. *"You are lycan, but it is not yet dark."*

Miranda froze. How in the hell could Lucifer be anywhere near here? Yet he had to be close since she could hear his mind voice.

"Well?" he pressed.

"They're trying to kill me," she protested. *"I didn't know what else to do."*

"Who would try to harm one of mine?" The voice was silky and seductive, but more gunfire nearly drowned out his words.

"Back to the road," he growled after she could hear again. Lucifer's rapidly shifting moods were legendary. *"Unless you've developed some new skills, you'll scarcely be able to defend yourself from where you stand."*

"Where are you?"

"Never mind about that. Just get moving."

How the hell could he know where she was—unless he was watching?

Tail twitching, nervous about yet one more angle to assimilate and deal with, she padded through the trees. She was closing on the road when the sound she'd been waiting for finally came. The snick of a car door. Pulling darkness about her, Miranda peered through the last of the tree cover. Ted stood next to his car half facing away from her, but she saw his profile clearly. Thick, brown hair fell to his shoulders. He was dressed in his usual western shirt, jeans, and cowboy boots.

"Miranda," he called once. Then again, louder. "Miranda, come on out. We can talk about this. I think you have something I want."

What the hell is he up to?

She stared at him from her vantage point, confused. She'd never bothered to talk with any of her victims before killing them. Judging the distance, she crept silently closer until a single spring would do it. Ted shouldered his gun and sprayed the woods with bullets. She knew she'd never get a better chance. The racket from his gun covered the noise she made as she leapt, knocking him into the dirt.

"Yes," he shouted, trying to turn to look at her. "Goddamn it, Miranda. Bite me."

Like hell I will, she thought, understanding why he'd called to her and knowing full well he had to die because he'd seen her in wolf form and could turn her in.

She barked a harsh laugh. Lucifer was most clear on the rules: no more lycans unless he approved them. Bounty hunters had all but wiped them out before Lucifer took over and changed things.

An unholy scream filled her ears after she sank her teeth into Ted's jugular, followed by a few shots when his dying fingers played over the trigger of the rifle sandwiched between his body and the ground. Miranda waited, her tongue lolling, as the last of Ted's life drained into the earth.

If Lucifer was close, and he had to be, she should offer him first feeding off her kill. She'd already broken one rule by shifting before full dark. She had no intention of breaking another. She clawed through Ted's pockets, but didn't find anything like orders. Leaving his body, she reared onto her hind legs and stared into the car. Nothing obvious in there, either. She'd need her human form to search.

Miranda had just reached for power to shift when a black and gray wolf with silver eyes strode toward her. She let the transformation magic scatter, faced Lucifer as a wolf, and inclined her head as a sign of respect. She'd seen him before at shifter gatherings, but never up close like this.

He smiled, his powerful jaws slightly ajar. Coming close, he rubbed noses with her. *"Nicely done,"* he chortled, low in the back of his throat. He licked her muzzle and sudden heat flared between her back legs.

I can't. What about Garen?

Miranda moved a few inches away and inclined her head again. Lucifer closed and licked her nose one more time, making his intentions crystal clear. Then he came round behind her and licked her vulva. Sexual tension ratcheted to a nearly unbearable level.

What am I saving myself for? Garen and I can never be together. Besides, I'm not sure I can say no to Lucifer. As far as she knew, no female lycan had ever refused the alpha.

Lucifer's tongue worked her vulva. Her muscles contracted. She wanted his cock inside her. Now. She dropped her head and squared her body on all four legs, twisting her tail aside to open a path.

Miranda was surprised by the sudden blaze of lust. She'd had sex with a few lycans, and they'd never made her so hot she thought she'd die if she didn't get them inside her. Human sex—the little she'd had with Garen—was far more complicated.

This was easy. She felt Lucifer's big paws on her shoulders and his weight on her. His teeth closed over the juncture of neck and shoulder. When he slid inside, she thought she'd never felt anything quite so delicious, and a low, hungry whine escaped her. His jaws tightened on her shoulder, and the pain made what was happening with her nether regions all the more intense. When her climax roared through her—and she came damned fast—she howled her joy to the forest. His guttural growls joined hers as his cock juddered deep within her body. The two of them stood, flanks heaving, for long moments as she came back into herself. It took a while for the swollen bulb at the base of his penis to shrink enough for them to separate.

After a time, he bent his muzzle and began to feed. She tried to join in, but he growled and snapped, so she knew this kill was not for her. The human part of her batted back irritation, but the wolf part understood. Lucifer was the pack leader, the alpha. He got whatever he wanted. No questions asked. Fading into the night shadows, she hunted. Each time she killed a small animal, the feel of living flesh and bone between her jaws excited her all over again, and she longed for Lucifer. Then she chided herself for foolishness. Chances of her ever even seeing him again outside of a gathering were unlikely.

Isn't that just great? I found a man I love. I can't have him. Now I found a wolf I'd like to get to know better, and I can't have him, either. Goddammit!

The journey back to town required planning. Lucifer was long gone when she returned to the scraps of her clothing and determined they were beyond salvage. That meant she'd be naked when she regained her human form. Not good. Turning, she ran fast through the last hours of the night, a dark streak in the gloom. Like all lycans, she had the ability to cloak her presence so long as it remained dark. Moonlight would've thrown a monkey wrench into things, but the night remained blessedly overcast and lessened her risk of discovery.

Approaching her building through a deserted alleyway, she probably gave a couple of drunks heart attacks. She heard them chittering to one another about *the wolf* as they raced to get away from her. After they sobered up—if they ever did—they'd likely chalk her up to a particularly bad case of d.t.'s.

Dawn caught her creeping into her apartment. Past the alleyway, she vaulted over the fence that surrounded her small patio, shifted, and dragged her tired human body inside and into a hot shower. Nursing a cup of instant coffee, Miranda tried to decide if she should show up at her desk at nine like she always did—unless she was off on assignment. She was feeling a touch remorseful about Ted and wondered what Garen's reaction would be to her report. She rolled her eyes. She could just envision the conversation.

Yeah, boss. You see, he was shooting at me, and I, uh, killed him. Never did get to the target you didn't tell me about...

Laughing wryly, she reminded herself there really were no friends in her particular line of work. Or anywhere else. She couldn't have human friends because of what she was. Lycan friends seemed out of the question, mostly since she only saw others like herself at the annual gathering and had no idea what any of them looked like in their human form. Miranda smiled sadly to herself.

Not really human. Not really a wolf. No place to call my own.

That decided it. Before she could sink into a morass of self-pity, she dried her hair, pulled on a long, wool dress, and caught a cab to work. When she got to her desk, there was a note from Garen telling her to come to his office immediately. Miranda blanched. *Shit.* Was the whole charade just going to start all over again? This was nothing like she expected. If she'd passed Rubicon

International's final test, wouldn't Garen have contacted her at home or by cell phone or something?

Yeah, right. Or had champagne delivered. Rein it in, sweetie.

Maybe coming in had been a mistake. She stared at Garen's note, handwritten on vellum in his strong hand. Suddenly wary, she considered walking out of the building and taking her chances. Calling on her wolf senses, she tried to puzzle out what to do. It was early yet. Even Garen wouldn't be expecting her for another half hour or so.

"You should go meet him." The voice in her head was faint but clear.

"Lucifer?"

She glanced around, but her office was empty. Miranda felt foolish. Did she just hallucinate Lucifer's voice?

"Whether I did or not, Garen's still my boss, and I need to do what he says," she muttered. Shoving her heavy hair out of her face, she stood and marched to her office door. Once through it, she headed for the private elevator toward the rear of the building, detouring back because she'd forgotten her key.

The elevator door opened smoothly, depositing her into the anteroom of Garen's lush office. She looked about, curious. She'd never been invited to the inner sanctum before. It was paneled from floor to ceiling in carved walnut. Carpet so thick she sank into it cushioned her shoes. Ornate crystal candelabra shed a muted light. Because she was alone, she took the time to look closely at the wood carvings and smiled when she noticed their espionage themes.

Despite a futile attempt at self-control, the heat from last night in the forest licked at her, and moisture slicked her thighs. She was actually reaching for herself when she realized what she was doing and made herself sit in a nearby chair. Her thighs pressed tightly together didn't help matters. She was just about to catch the elevator back down so she could duck into a restroom to take care of her little problem, when the door to the inner office opened, and Garen strode purposefully toward her. She got to her feet.

His brows were drawn together, and he looked serious. "I see you got my note."

"Yes, sir."

Her arousal crashed and burned as she wondered what was going on. Did he still want her dead? Would she have to fight him? Maybe she was *supposed* to die last night, and he was planning to finish her off. The wolf part of her liked the prospect of a brawl, and she had to force down a growl so he wouldn't hear it. Another part of her, the part that wanted nothing more than to dive into the comfort of his arms, was devastated by the prospect of having to fight him.

She remembered a point one of her first Army drill sergeants had hammered home. *There are no friends in espionage work. Trust no one.* Miranda tugged the tattered remnants of her heart together and met Garen's gaze.

"Report."

She straightened her shoulders. "Ted tried to kill me. Um, actually he may have just been trying to lure me out of my hiding place with automatic weapon fire. When I outmaneuvered him and established the upper hand, he begged me to bite him."

"And?" Garen raised an arched brow, creating a question mark.

"It's against the rules. No more lycans without Lucifer's permission."

"Who's Lucifer?"

Aha, so he's just a wolf shifter and not a lycan...

"The lycans' alpha."

She pushed straggling strands of hair out of her face and sucked in a deep breath. "You probably already know, but I killed Ted."

"It's exactly what you were supposed to do. He wasn't one of us." Garen's expression hardened. "He told us he was, but he wasn't, so he had to go."

"He was my assignment yesterday?"

Garen nodded and grinned at her, but his eyes were cold. "Smart cookie. It's one of the things I've always liked about you, Miss Miller."

Something Garen said—*Ted told us he was like us, but he wasn't*—sank in. Understanding flickered. "Rubicon International is all... those like us?"

He nodded, a damped-down smirk on his face. "Uh-huh. It's not like we can advertise for shifters and werewolves, but there is, shall we say, a natural sorting process. I wasn't even quite certain about you—until the night at the Index cabin."

Miranda eyed him speculatively. "What happens next?"

"You become a part of the inner circle, and whole new worlds will open. We hold incredible power."

She was intrigued but wasn't certain what to ask, so she remained silent.

He extracted a knife from one of his pockets. "Come closer."

Miranda eyed the knife, unsure about Garen's motives again. She shook her head, realizing how tired she was. "Why?"

"It's necessary to create a blood bond. All fully vetted agents are bound to me—and to Rubicon International—by blood." He drew his brows together. "When did you stop trusting me?"

"When you sent me out by myself yesterday without instructions."

Awk. I sound like a whiny ten-year-old.

"You're not thinking. I couldn't tell you I didn't trust Ted. You needed to assess the situation on your own and make your own decisions. What if I'd been wrong about him? I'd have smeared an agent's reputation for nothing and made it impossible for any of the rest of you to work with him." Garen hesitated. "It's sort of like going from enlisted man to officer in the service. The main difference is you need to think for yourself and bear the consequences for your decisions."

"I understand. At least I think I do."

He cocked his head to one side. "You're still here, Miranda, so it appears I judged your capabilities well. Hold out your hand." His voice was stern. He brandished the small blade and made a shallow cut in the meaty part of her thumb, then did the same thing to his own hand.

Once their blood mingled, he handed her a gauze square and some tape. "Go home and get some sleep," he growled.

"What about San Ysidro?"

"Be back here at seventeen hundred. We'll complete the final assignments then. The team pulls out tomorrow, and you'll need to be sharper than you are at the moment."

CHAPTER 12

Garen thrust his hands deep into his pockets to keep from pulling Miranda against him. He wanted to hold her and comfort her and tell her he was sorry, but there hadn't been a better way to test both her and Ted at the same time. He'd given Ted an assignment, but the target had been bogus. He'd been nearly certain Ted would try to convince Miranda to provide the bite that would save his bacon at Rubicon International. He'd been equally certain Miranda wouldn't rise to the bait.

She staggered from weariness as she walked out of his office. "You're sure I can't send a car and a driver to see you home?" he called after her.

"Nah." She didn't even turn around. "I'll be fine."

He sank into a soft chair and shut his eyes. He shouldn't have shown himself as a wolf the previous night. He'd been banking on the muting that meant they didn't reason well in their wolf forms.

Yeah, I tossed the dice and won, but I'm a fucking fool.

Not only had he trotted out of the woods, big as you please, he'd let his lust run wild and mated with her. All he'd meant to do was watch from a distance to make certain she was all right.

Even though it was obvious she had things under control, he

couldn't leave well enough alone. No, he had to march right up to her, lick her snout, and... Once he'd allowed her to see him, desperation took over. He wanted her more intensely than he'd ever wanted another lycan, but he also needed to divert her so she wouldn't recognize his scent from their brief moments together as lycans in Index. The best diversion he knew met his other objective. He pumped out pheromones, obliterating every other scent in the air with his hunger for her.

A tongue of jealousy intruded. Miranda didn't realize he and Lucifer were one and the same. She'd ceded to Lucifer's lust without so much as an eye bat. "What the hell was she supposed to do?" he muttered. "Tell the lycan leader no?" Female wolves didn't tell him no at gatherings. It had been one of the sideline benefits of being their alpha until he'd become so besotted with Miranda he didn't want another female—human or shifter—within fifty paces of him.

He pushed out of the chair and settled at his desk. Maybe if he worked on details for San Ysidro, he'd be able to relegate Miranda to a back burner for a while. He was breaking yet another of rules and going with the team to the ISL compound. Normally, Garen stayed behind at headquarters. That way, he could deploy more troops or oversee extractions if things went to shit.

I don't have to go.

Yes, I do. There's no way I'm turning Miranda loose that far from me in a dangerous situation.

He stared at the monitor, seeing the intricate flow pattern of their attack, but unable to concentrate on it. Instead, he saw Miranda's face, cheeks flushed with passion, eyes gleaming warmly at him in her high-cheekboned face.

I've got to talk with someone. I'm about as worthless as a caged monkey.

Garen tugged his cell phone out of a pocket and punched the series of numbers that would connect him to Lars, the only one who knew about his alter ego, Lucifer.

The phone only rang a couple of times. "Greetings, my friend. I did not expect to hear from you so soon."

"Is your connection secure?"

"Of course." Lars sounded hurt. "I am not into taking unnecessary chances. What do you need?"

"An ear."

Lars' breath whistled through the cellular system. "That bad, eh?"

"Worse." Garen sketched out what had transpired since Lars left Index, omitting some of the gritty details of his inability to do anything but lust after Miranda. When he couldn't think of any more to say, he fell silent.

"So." The single word held a universe of meaning. "You have had sex with her in human form and shifted form. Have you truly forgotten the significance of that?"

Garen's eyes widened, and the wind punched out of his lungs. Not only had he forgotten, it never crossed his mind when he'd taken the fateful step and sunk his wolf cock inside her wolf vulva. He opened his mouth to say something, but it was so dry words wouldn't come. He took a sip of cold coffee, sloshed it around in his mouth before swallowing, and tried again.

"I, uh… Let's just say it was far from front and center in my mind. The main thing I was worried about was her connecting Lucifer to my wolf that she'd already met in Index. Ach, Christ! I truly have screwed myself."

Lars chuckled, but the sound lacked mirth. "Selfish to the core, as always. It is one of the reasons we get along so well. What about Miranda? She deserves to know. She will be experiencing the same longing and hopelessness since she does not expect the two of you will ever be a couple."

"She's right. We can't be."

"Why not?" Lars asked with characteristic Teutonic pragmatism.

"She works for Rubicon International."

"Easily fixed. She could work for me at the European branch. Or she could not work at all. It is not as if you could not provide for her."

"She'd never accede to being taken care of."

"Old friend. If I were next to you, I would slap you. You have no idea what she will do with the information, but you must tell her. It is a breach in the covenant that governs our kind if you do not."

Garen squeezed his eyes shut. He had to think about something else or his brain would explode. "Are you in the middle of something, or are you free to help with a project?"

Lars snorted. "What a rapid shift of topics. I might be able to provide assistance. It would depend when you needed me—and for what."

"I will scramble the details and get them to you electronically. How soon could you get to southern California?"

Silence. Finally, he said, "Forty-eight hours. I believe I will fly commercial this time."

"The next briefing is at seventeen hundred hours later today. I'll funnel you in via webcam."

Lars rattled off an Internet address. Garen jotted it down and said, "Thank you," only to find Lars had disconnected. It had been kind of him not to chastise Garen. As it was, his conscience writhed in agony—yet if he was honest, Garen knew he'd make the same choice again. Miranda was damn near irresistible. Even if she ran to the ends of the world to get away from him, he'd always cherish the little time they'd spent together.

He laid the phone aside, his mouth curving into a soft smile. By making love with Miranda in both their forms, he'd sealed the mate bond. She was his—and he was hers—forever. Normally shifters discussed these things before taking such a drastic step. Hundreds of years ago, before shifters had been driven underground, he'd taken care who he screwed to avoid making an ineradicable mistake. Beyond that, he'd been lucky. He'd known the odd lycan who'd been snared in a mate bond without their permission, which was why there were prohibitions against such things.

The repercussions of what he'd done sank in. Torn between delight he'd actually bound them together and fear she wouldn't want either him or the bond, he recognized he had to talk with her —explain everything—and let the chips fall where they would. It was worse not to tell her than for her to know he was Lucifer.

His jaw clenched with tension; so did his gut. San Ysidro. Miranda had to have her wits about her to carry out her delicate part in the operation. In many ways, it was her undertaking. She'd unearthed the location and planned the maneuver to infiltrate it. She couldn't be distracted by mate bonds and justifiable anger at him.

"I'll tell her just as soon as it's over with," he muttered to his empty office. "I'll make reservations out on one of the islands so we'll have privacy, and I'll fess up and take my lumps."

He shut his eyes for a moment. If she rejected him—and she could easily be angry enough to do so—the mate bond would still be there. It would mean she could never love another. Neither could he.

I can't believe I was that stupid. He clenched his hands into fists until his nails dug into his palms. *Just because I was so taken with her, she was all I could think about, it was deucedly unfair of me not to tell her the truth and offer her a choice.*

Yeah, right. How could I have done that? I didn't even realize it myself until Lars threw it in my face.

He gritted his teeth together so hard he thought they might shatter. Love for Miranda coursed through him, along with a savage desire to protect her from the consequences of his poor choices.

He picked up the phone again and dialed an out-of-the-way bed-and-breakfast inn on Bainbridge Island. He'd stayed there before when he needed to get away from everything. The proprietors were shifters—retired RI agents—who knew how to keep their mouths shut. It was the perfect place to take Miranda—if she agreed to go. He glanced at a calendar. Ten days should just about wrap up San Ysidro.

"Belle Maison Inn. How may I help you?"

"Lore? Garen here. I'd like to make reservations for your honeymoon cabin starting..."

~

Miranda glanced around the large oval conference room table at RI's headquarters. She'd slept like a dead thing from mid-morning until her phone alarm woke her at three-thirty. Nine agents ranged around the table. Lars had joined them via web link. Garen sat at the head of the table. She made a concerted effort not to look at him. Though she'd struggled with her feelings for him before, those tussles were nothing compared with the drive she felt to jump from her chair and throw herself into his arms.

San Ysidro will be a good break. At least I'll get away for a few days, and I can try to put everything into perspective.

"So." Miranda stood, arms crossed over her chest, at the opposite end of the table from Garen. "Once I'm in, I'll do what I can to marshal the women—and men, if there are any."

An older agent named Jordan said, "There will be. ISL traffics in candy for the gay boys too. Be particularly careful. Watch out for Stockholm Syndrome. Some of those human slaves may well have bonded with their captors." He pushed thick, gray hair back from his face. His brown eyes didn't miss much.

"Yes," Nadine seconded. She ran slender fingers through her close-cropped red hair and scowled. "They'd turn you into ISL's thugs in a second if they saw you as a threat. No matter how bad things seem to you, the merchandise has adapted to it."

Jordan grunted. "It's human nature to cling to the status quo."

"Good advice. Thanks." Miranda tried to smile, but all she managed was a grimace. She'd pushed for this operation, but now that it was getting close, she was scared. "I'll do what I can to disable the locks and alarms. Once that's done, I'll alert the team."

"And we'll storm the fortress." Garen's arms were crossed over his chest too.

"It will take me a few days. Maybe as much as a week," Miranda said. "When I first get inside—assuming I'm successful—I'm going to aim for invisibility. The last thing I want to do is make waves so they'll notice the new acquisition."

"What will you do if the men want to fuck you?" Jordan asked bluntly.

"I thought I'd tell them I just finished treatment for gonorrhea. They'll need to have a doctor clear me."

"That won't slow them down," Garen muttered, looking like he wanted to kill something. "They'll use condoms."

"Maybe I can tell them I just had an abortion, and I can't have sex for two weeks."

"Better." He nodded. Something intense flared behind his eyes, but he hooded them before she got a close enough look to identify it.

"Go over your story again," Nadine prodded. "I want to look for holes."

Miranda nodded. "I'm going to make the rounds of the border strip clubs looking for work. Each place, I'll tell anyone who seems even peripherally interested about my Mexican in-laws dumping their gringo daughter-in-law north of the border after they fleeced me for my car and bank account." She sucked in a breath. "All I have left is my passport and driver's license. I'm hungry, and I really need to work. My own family's all dead."

"Work on your language," Garen snapped. "You won't be using words like *peripherally*."

"I know that." Irritation scoured her nerves. She pressed her tongue against her teeth. "I'm gonna tell 'em I done dropped out of school in Tombstone. Needin' to lay a bit by so's I kin git back there."

"If you do not talk very much, you can probably pull it off." Lars, who'd been so silent she'd forgotten about him, spoke through the web link's mic. "I am used to listening for subtle nuance in language. Your fake accent is broken, uneven, but it is unlikely any of the ISL people will have my level of sophistication."

"Have you firmed up when you'll arrive?" Garen turned toward the wall screen and faced Lars.

"Affirmative. Three a.m. Thursday morning. I leave immediately after this conference. I would already be en route, but I needed secure conference capabilities."

"All right. We'll move into position Thursday midday. Lars will meet us in San Ysidro. No point in him coming to Seattle first."

"Are the rest of us still traveling by private jet?" one of the other agents asked.

Garen nodded. "We leave tomorrow at eleven hundred hours from Boeing field. I have agents packing the plane as we speak." He nailed her with his intense blue gaze. "Miranda."

"Sir." She managed to look alert without exactly looking at him.

"The blood bond means you'll be able to communicate telepathically over distances, not just if one of us is right next to you. It also means you'll be able to use telepathy in your human form. We're going to spend the next hour practicing, so you get to know what our mind voices sound like."

Her eyes widened and darted from agent to agent. Right. All of them were some kind of shifter. She wanted to ask for more information, but long habit kept her lips sealed.

"I will sign off," Lars said. "See you all soon. Here is to our success. The world will be a better place without Roulan and his filthy operation." Lars' handsome face broke into a grin on the video monitor. "Correction. It is already a better place without Roulan, thanks to Miranda. A preemptive strike, which further weakens his business, is a positive move. If we can cripple their income stream and free at least a few of the captives, we will truly celebrate."

"I've always loved your optimism." Garen smiled. "See you soon." He swung his piercing gaze around the table. "Mind speech only."

A blast of voices battered her. Miranda put her hands over her ears and then laughed at her gaffe. *"One at a time, please. Let me get used to you one at a time."* She thought the words and pushed them, much as she did in her lycan form. Everyone must've heard her because the cacophony in her head died down.

She was tired by the time Garen dismissed them with instructions when to meet at Boeing field the next day. All of them but her. He'd requested that she remain. Miranda's stomach twisted uncomfortably. What did he want now? Wasn't it enough he was coming along on this venture—her project—to babysit her? At least she'd put some distance between them while she was in the ISL compound.

Gee. Since when does being scared half out of my wits and forced to be vigilant even when I'm sleeping look better than spending time with a man who shatters me every time he looks at me?

Since I'm out of control when I'm with him. All I want to do is cozy up in his arms and fuck him and let him take care of me. If I spend too much time with him, I'll end up a weak, mewling hausfrau baking cakes and raising kids.

"Miss Miller?" Garen had an odd look on his face. She remembered the blood bond and wondered just how much of her mental process was available to him. Just to be safe, she shrouded her thoughts.

"Yes?"

He closed the distance between them and drew her into his arms. She tried to be wooden, to resist, but found herself leaning into his warmth and solidness. She tilted her face for a kiss, but he just looked at her with sad eyes. "Be careful. Do not take any untoward chances. If things seem to be going south—and you'll know, you have good instincts—get the hell out of there. I don't care if you have to crawl out a fucking drain pipe. Do not remain if there's even a hint you've been compromised."

"Okay. I understand."

"Do you?" He tipped her chin and forced her to look right at him. "They'll kill you without a second thought. These people are merciless." He closed both arms around her again and held her close. His next words were whispered, and so low she had to strain to hear them. "I don't particularly want to live in a world without you in it, Miranda. Be vigilant."

He let her go. The places his body had pressed against hers felt cold and lonely. He turned away and gathered things into his briefcase. "Dismissed."

"But—"

"Get out of here, Miranda, before I do something I promised I wouldn't."

She picked up her backpack, which doubled as a briefcase, and walked heavily from the room. It was one of the hardest things she'd ever done. She wanted Garen. If things went to shit in San Ysidro and she died, she knew she'd regret not having shared one last night with him.

Miranda shook her head hard and activated the electronic keypad to let herself into the stairwell. "I do not need emotional complications." She spoke aloud to reinforce her resolve. And then she repeated the words. By the time she got to street level and a taxi stand, she'd said them over at least twenty times, but she still wasn't convinced.

CHAPTER 13

*M*iranda took a slug from the water bottle tucked in her over-the-shoulder bag. Unseasonable heat made what few clothes she was wearing stick to her, and sweat ran down her sides. Even though it was on the U.S. side of the border, San Ysidro was bleak and depressing. Trash clotted the gutters of its illegal red-light district. Brothels, masquerading as strip clubs, lined both sides of the street. She'd been in half a dozen clubs and heard the same thing: come back tonight. Apparently no one who could make a decision was available at five in the afternoon.

Though she hadn't seen any of them, the rest of the team was in proximity. They checked in telepathically with one another every hour if nothing was going on, more frequently if one of them had something to report.

"I'm heading back to alpha one," she sent. *"I'll hit the beat again around twenty-one hundred."*

"Señorita."

Miranda plodded toward the boarding house where she'd bought a week's worth of lodging. No reason not to take a break, have a bite to eat, and gear up for the evening.

"Señorita, stop."

Surely he can't be talking to me.

She glanced around the nearly deserted street. A swarthy man draped in a colorful serape motioned to her from one of the clubs she'd wandered into. Miranda tapped her chest and cocked her head to one side. She'd be damned if she'd shout back at him.

He nodded enthusiastically, so she trotted toward him. Her pulse quickened. Maybe her luck was about to change. She struck a seductive pose right next to the tall, dark man with greasy hair. "Yes?"

"I talk to boss man. You have place to stay?" His Mexican accent was so thick it wasn't easy to understand him.

Miranda shook her head. "No money. It's why I went in your bar huntin' work."

He beamed at her, displaying yellowed teeth with several missing. "This your lucky day, señorita. Come with me."

"Scratch my last transmission. Things are popping."

Miranda shifted her weight to her other foot and pushed her breasts forward. "Where you takin' me, handsome?"

"Special house. You stay there."

Miranda did her best to look distressed. "I told you. I got no money to pay rent."

"No rent. Free for pretty señoritas like you." As if sensing her hesitation, he added, "Food too. You hungry?"

Miranda nodded. A tear slid down one cheek. *Shit! I should have gone to Juilliard.* "Um, I'm just not sure about coming with you. Where is this place?"

"Not far. Car coming." Beady eyes turned away from her and scanned the street. "Just turn corner."

A shiny black Cadillac motored right toward them and screeched to a halt. Her Mexican companion tugged the back door open. A quick glance showed her the inner rear door handles had been removed. No point in trapping herself unnecessarily. She hung back. "I get carsick. Need to ride in the front. Or I could walk if you'd give me an address." She smiled brightly.

The Mexican looked uncertain. He leaned into the car and spoke with the driver in a Mexican patois of gutter Spanish mixed with a few English words. Miranda felt the driver's gaze settle on her. She did her best to look harmless and sexy. It worked.

The driver leaned over and pushed the front passenger door open. "Get in," he grunted. His English was considerably better than the other man's.

Miranda settled herself, taking care to flash an expanse of thigh before she tugged her long, slit skirt together. She ignored her seatbelt. The driver wasn't wearing one. "Where we goin'?"

The car lurched forward, hung a U-turn, and accelerated. "You'll find out when we get there. It ain't far. The girls walk from there to work."

Miranda assumed *work* was where they'd just been. "It's kind of you to help a stranger—" she began.

"Quiet. I ain't interested in conversation. Or sex, so keep your skin to yourself."

Well, that's a relief.

The taciturn driver was balding and at least fifty pounds overweight. He looked like he came from somewhere in the Mediterranean, but his accent was pure Brooklyn.

Five minutes later, he pulled up in front of the ISL compound. Miranda peered out the window and pointed. "Is that it? You were right. It wasn't far at all."

"Get out. Knock on the glass door." His brow furrowed. "You got any stuff?"

"Nope. In-laws dumped me. All I got's in here." She patted her shoulder bag and pursed her lips, aiming for an expression between sad and angry. "They would've taken everything, but I fought 'em for my bag."

"Fine, sister. I don't give a fuck. Just didn't want you leaving anything in here. Get out. Taxi ride's over."

She walked smartly to the double glass doors and pushed. Locked, which wasn't a surprise. Once she got in, getting out would take some doing. She'd be surprised if they let her out to work, or do anything else, until they were certain she wouldn't make a break for freedom and turn them in.

"I said knock," the driver yelled out his window.

Miranda raised a fist and knocked.

It took a while, but an overweight woman with gray hair pulled into a bun eventually clumped down a staircase at the far end of the dingy lobby. She pulled a ring of keys from her belt and undid a series of deadbolts. Wires were visible in the glass. An alarm system.

The woman pulled the door open. "Needing a place to stay, are you?"

Miranda nodded. "I got no money."

The woman waved her to silence. "No matter. We'll take care of you. Come on with me, I'll take you to your room. Dinner's in fifteen. We'll pass the dining room along the way so you can see where it is."

MIRANDA SAT at a trestle table filled with chattering women. Children ran through the dining room as if they owned the place. If she hadn't known better, the ISL compound would've looked like a dormitory for unwed mothers. Her roommate, a sullen Asian woman with doll-pretty features, hadn't said three words to her. Miranda had tried to say hello and been met with, "English no good." The woman, Tara, sat across the room with a gaggle of other Asians.

Miranda scanned the dining room. Perhaps fifty women—and a few very attractive men—filled the tables. Other men, presumably guards, milled around the room. The bulge of weapons showed beneath their jackets. It wasn't obvious, but she knew the outline of a semiautomatic pistol, no matter how subtle.

Adrenaline thrummed. It was hard to choke down the stringy, dried-out pork chop on her plate. The mashed potatoes had the consistency of gluey cardboard. A dollop of applesauce tasted watered down. She took a sip of over-sweetened iced tea.

"Hey." The woman nearest her jabbed Miranda. "You gonna eat that?"

"Probably not. I'm a little nervous, being new and all. Is this a, um, whorehouse? Is that why they feed us and give us a place to sleep?"

The woman—actually she didn't look a day over sixteen—had spiky red hair and a face full of freckles. She rolled her green eyes. "They ain't sat down with you yet. You'll get the skinny soon enough. Your dinner?"

Miranda smiled. "You can have it. What's your name?"

"Becky." The young woman sidled closer. Her gaze skittered around the room. "It's against the rules," she hissed into Miranda's ear. "You got to eat what they set in front of you. Think they got the calories all planned out or something. Just enough to keep us fit enough to work."

"I'm Miranda. I'll just reach over you for the tea."

Becky got the picture. In the split seconds while Miranda's body acted as a shield, she transferred the meat and half the potatoes to her plate. The girl ate hungrily. Miranda tried to choke down more of the potatoes, but they were truly vile. She was just contemplating returning to her room when one of the guards headed toward her table.

Miranda looked away and took another mouthful. *Damn!* Had he seen her sleight of hand to allow Becky more food?

A heavy hand settled on her shoulder. "Come with me."

Miranda sucked in a breath. "I, um, I'm not quite done eating yet."

The guard snorted, blowing spittle in her face. "Ask me if I care, bitch. I ain't gonna wait on you." The hand on her shoulder slid forward and settled over one of her breasts. Miranda cursed her formfitting top, which left nothing to the imagination.

"Hey, sister." Becky nudged her. "It'll be okay. It's just

orientation. Happens to all of us when we first get here. They won't put you to work for a few days. Got to get your health clearance back first."

Miranda ducked from beneath the guard's hand. She longed to grab hold of it and break his wrist. It'd be easy enough so long as she got the angle right. "Okay. Okay," she said. "I'm coming."

The guard followed her out of the dining room. "Left. To the end of the hall."

Miranda gathered as much intel as she could. Her room was the opposite way, so she hadn't been down this hallway before. It was lined with closed doors. At the end of the hall, the guard tapped on one. It opened almost immediately. He shoved her inside, and the door snicked shut behind her.

She kept her eyes on her feet. This wasn't the place to look anything but cowed.

"Timid one, eh?"

Miranda looked up for a moment. She tried for a deer-in-the-headlights look before she studied the carpet again. A stunning man strode across the room and took a seat behind a carved wooden desk, facing her. Dark hair framed his clean-shaven face and fell to his shoulders. Dark eyes held cunning and a keen intelligence. Tailored clothes set off his broad-shouldered frame to perfection.

Her nostrils flared. Expensive aftershave applied with a too-liberal hand filled the smallish room that looked like a study.

"What's the matter, sweetheart? Cat got your tongue?"

"No. Just nervous, I guess."

"You can look at me. I don't bite."

Ha! I'll just bet you don't.

She met his gaze. "It was, um, kind to take me in since I don't got much. I, er, understand I got to work. I'd applied at some of them clubs—"

He waved her to silence. "I said you could look at me. I do the talking, Miss—" he raised a questioning brow.

"Oh. I done forgot my manners." She ginned up a hangdog

expression. "Miranda Buckley. Guess it's really missus, 'ceptin' my husband threw me out. Buckley's my family name—"

"For Christ's sake, woman. Shut up."

"Sorry." She looked down.

"You'll work in the clubs starting in a week or so. Maybe here. Maybe in another city. We make those decisions. Eat everything you're given. No sex with the other residents—male or female."

She ginned up a hopeful look. "When I've earned me some money, can I go shopping? I ain't got much in the way of clothes."

"Perhaps. It will be a while before we trust you to leave any of our facilities on your own."

"Huh?" Her forehead creased. "I'm not followin' you, sir."

"What are you, brain-damaged? No one gets something for nothing, Miranda Buckley. You belong to us."

"F-for how long, uh, sir?"

"Forever, Miranda. Stand still. I'm going to take some blood out of your arm. We need to test you for VD, hepatitis, and HIV before we turn you loose on our customers." He opened a drawer and pulled out a syringe.

She drew back. No way was she letting him stick her with whatever might be in the syringe under the guise of drawing blood. "Ain't that supposed to be like wrapped in plastic or somethin'? 'Sides, I'm clean. Just had an abortion, and they did all them tests."

"Really?" He advanced toward her, syringe in hand.

"Yes, sir. I got no call to lie to you." Miranda backed toward the door and readied herself to fight. "I am not okay with you stickin' me with that needle. I ain't no junkie. Hate needles, and that one don't look clean."

Maybe something in her face changed his mind. He inclined his head slightly. "The nurse will be by tomorrow. She's here once a week. I'll have her drop by to get your blood."

Miranda squared her shoulders. "How's about I call the clinic and have them fax all that test shit here?"

His narrowed eyes turned into fiery, dark holes. "No. Better get used to the word. Now get out of my sight."

Miranda scuttled out of the room. The same guard waited just beyond the door for her and escorted her back to her room. Tara stood in front of a mirror applying makeup, presumably for the night's activities. The guard sashayed into the room and pinched her butt before he left, slamming the door behind him.

The second he was gone, Tara's porcelain-doll face twisted into a grimace. "Bad man. Rules say no sex."

Miranda thought about clarifying that the no sex rule only applied to residents. Instead, she stretched out on her twin bed. Maybe, once everyone left for the evening, she could do a bit of prowling.

Tara padded over to her. "You lucky. No work tonight."

"How'd you end up here?" Miranda kept her voice low. She didn't see a mic anywhere, but that didn't mean there wasn't one tucked in a crevice somewhere.

Tara shook her head. Shiny black hair fell in her face. "You no want know. Once here. No leave. Family think me dead." A tear formed in one almond eye and slid down her cheekbone. Her tiny hands curled into fists. "No cry," she hissed. "Punish for cry."

Miranda wanted to hold out her arms to comfort the woman but didn't. Closed-circuit television was a distinct possibility. Once Tara left, she'd check the room over. "Aw, it's probably not as bad as you think."

"Is worse than bad dream. You just get here. Not know." She lifted a corner of her kimono-esque top and displayed a bruise that ran around her entire torso. "Men," she snapped. "Bastards. You find out soon enough." She gathered a small bag and trudged out of the room.

Miranda glanced at the time. Nine.

"Report," echoed in her head. Garen's voice. Mind speech couldn't mask how worried he was.

"I'm in. No work for a week, but I shouldn't be here that long. Fifty

residents. Maybe ten children. I've seen six guards and the man who runs things."

"Describe him," Lars cut in.

Once she was done, she heard a hissing intake of breath. "I suppose he could have a clone, but I'm nearly certain his name is Alejandro," Garen told her. "He's one of ISL's top agents and extremely dangerous. Do not underestimate him. Do not turn your back on him. He's a mountain lion shifter. I've fought him when he was in that form before." A hesitation, then, "Do I make myself clear?"

"Abundantly. Once everyone has left for the evening, I plan to take a little look around."

"Report at the top of every hour."

"Understood."

Miranda waited until nearly ten. In the intervening time, she went over her room carefully and found both a video camera and a microphone.

I'll have to find a way to tell Tara to keep her mouth shut. No wonder they're beating her.

She took a shower, got back into her clothes, and doused the lights, grateful when the camera didn't light up with an infrared beam. That meant it was either off or it couldn't transmit in the absence of light. After her ten p.m. check-in, she went to the door and turned the knob. Miranda was shocked it actually opened. She'd been certain they'd lock her in. She eyed the doorknob and doorjamb. Insofar as she could tell, the door didn't lock—from either side.

Makes sense. The building is locked, so there's no reason to lock us in our rooms.

She looked up and down the empty, dimly lit corridor hunting for closed-circuit cameras now that she knew what they looked like. Sure enough, they were mounted at about shoulder level. She was fairly certain if she dropped to the floor and belly-crawled, she'd be beneath their electronic beam.

Miranda dialed in her lycan hearing and stood absolutely still.

Maybe the guards had gone with the prisoners. The compound was quiet. Her room was on the middle of three floors. The dining room and the room where she'd met Alejandro were on the first floor. An idea blossomed. She shut the door noiselessly and retreated to her room's single window. It was large enough to crawl through. She inspected the sill and sides. Wired. She'd expected as much, but had to check. She peered into the darkness but couldn't see enough. Anyway, it didn't matter. The window wasn't of any use as an escape route if she couldn't open it without alerting someone.

Back to Plan A.

Miranda crept from her room, dropped to her belly, and slithered to one of several internal stairwells. Adrenaline made her nerves tingle. She inspected the stairwell door carefully. It was the same one she'd gone through on her way down to dinner. If it was wired, she couldn't see any evidence. Mouth dry, she opened it and stepped through, expecting to hear the pound of footsteps. She had a story ready about going to the kitchen for a snack, but she didn't need it since no one materialized.

She headed to the top floor. Maybe there'd be a way to access the roof. If nothing else, she'd get the lay of the land. She had hours before the human slaves—and their keepers—would return. She'd just opened the door at the top of the stairwell when someone yanked it out of her hand and slammed it against the wall. She shrank back, but she wasn't fast enough. A hand snaked out and grabbed her upper arm.

Maybe I can play innocent. After all, I'm still inside the building. It's not as if I jimmied a window or an outside door.

"Ouch. You're hurting me. I couldn't sleep and decided to walk around a little."

The hand dragged her up the last step and into the upstairs hallway. Alejandro's patrician features came into view. He scowled at her, looking like he wanted to wring her neck. "Nice try, Miss Buckley. Or was that Miss Miller?"

Her heart sped up. "I'm sure I have no idea what you're talkin' about, sir."

"Like hell you don't. Although I must admit I expected you'd at least try to blend in for twenty-four hours before you put your spy training to good use. Green Berets, wasn't it, Miss Miller?" he continued, silkily smooth. "I'm sure you don't remember me, but I was part of your last operation in Afghanistan—on the other side, of course." The hand that wasn't holding onto her hauled off and slapped her hard, dead across the face.

"I've been compromised."

"I heard that. In fact, I've heard every mind transmission you've sent since you got here. How many are out there?"

"How?" she countered. "I don't have a blood bond with you."

"I have my ways, and they're no concern of yours." He sneered, displaying lengthened canines. He might still be human, but his cat was close to the surface.

Miranda plowed ahead, leveraging time so Garen could get to her. "If you can hear me, you should be able to hear them too."

He slapped her again, hard enough to rattle her teeth. "I asked you a question," he gritted through clenched teeth.

"You actually think I'll tell you?" Miranda borrowed his phrase from earlier. "What are you, brain-damaged?" She employed an aikido maneuver, using his strength against him, and wrenched herself out of his grasp. Hands raised, she stared at him from a few feet away. "So are we just going to duke it out here in the third-floor hallway?"

He shrugged. "We could. Or I could shoot you. It would save everyone a lot of trouble."

She stared at his heavily muscled frame draped in black linen trousers and a snug black sweater. "I don't see a gun."

"I didn't say when I'd shoot you. There's nowhere to run. Even if you elude me tonight, which isn't likely, I'll track you down."

Need to keep him talking. Maybe he'll make a mistake.

"So you remember me from the Middle East. Any particular reason?" She inhaled deeply and kept her body loose and fluid.

The leer turned into a snarl. For a moment, she saw his cat features and readied herself to shift if he did. "You took out half a dozen of my best men. Surely you remember. You were so high I expected you to drink their blood."

"I killed a lot of people in the field. Sorry. I don't remember which ones belonged to you."

"Bitch." He feinted toward her.

She moved away, her gaze never leaving him. A knife materialized in his hand.

Damn. Must've been up his sleeve.

The wicked, serrated blade gleamed dully. He lunged at her. She aimed a high kick at his wrist. The knife clattered to the linoleum floor, but he grabbed her ankle with his other hand. She pivoted but lost her balance and landed heavily on her ass.

Miranda drove her free foot into his crotch. He grunted with pain and let go of her. She leapt to her feet, intent on securing the knife, but he moved between her and her objective much faster than she expected.

This is bullshit. I have nothing to lose.

In a matter of seconds, she shifted, hoping the shimmer would blind him—and shield her.

Please, please don't let him get hold of the knife.

Before her cells were totally done with the transformation, Miranda launched herself, expecting to feel the sting of his blade. It never came. Instead of a human body, her wolf collided with a mountain cat. A boom sounded from below them. She hoped it was Garen and the team.

Teeth sank into her shoulder. Claws raked her fur and dug into her flanks. She closed her jaws over his carotid. Blood geysered, showering her.

All I have to do is hang on. If that explosion was Garen blowing the door, he should be here soon.

Beyond reason, the cat that should be dying, continued to claw at her, raking long holes in her flanks. Icy realization slammed home, along with hot blood drenching her fur.

Aw shit, loving Garen is way more important than my field career. Will I live long enough to lay eyes on him and tell him?

The air grew rank with blood and animal smells. Spots swam in front of her eyes, and she understood that lots of the blood running down the hallway had to be hers. The mountain cat's body went limp beneath her. Fearing treachery, she dug her teeth deeper.

"Goddammit, Garen. Third floor. Now."

Consciousness flirted with her, but the courtship was brief. Despite her best efforts, it slipped away.

CHAPTER 14

Garen paced restlessly across the street from the compound. Lars had tried to dissuade him from such close surveillance by pointing out they could blow Miranda's cover if they were visible, but Garen hadn't listened. "We have to be close," he'd insisted. "What if something goes wrong? A few minutes could make all the difference." He hated the idea of her inside that hellhole.

Should've put my foot down and just told her no.

She hadn't reported at midnight. It was thirty minutes past when he heard her telepathic call for help.

Thank Christ I made her a full agent and bound her with blood.

"Everyone. Plan C. Go, go, go. Five, four, three..."

He'd set a few discreet globs of plastique around the front door as soon as the slaves and their keepers left for the evening. Garen activated the detonator while he mobilized the team. And hoped like hell the entire building didn't collapse. As soon as the door gave, he vaulted through it, hit the first stairwell he found, and raced to the top floor.

The smell of blood—rivers of it—hit him full-on long before he got there. Panic shattered his nerves. If anything happened to

Miranda—his woman, his *mate*—he'd never forgive himself. Never. He blew through the stairwell door into the upper hallway. Empty. Dread lent speed to his legs. He pounded down the hallway and around an *L* corner.

"Motherfucker!" Garen barely recognized the shriek as his.

Miranda lay still as death on the floor in wolf form, her body tangled with Alejandro's. The two were locked in mortal combat. Neither moved. Blood pooled around them and ran in every direction. Garen threw himself atop the shifters' bodies and pried Alejandro's teeth and claws out of Miranda. It was harder to loosen her jaws from the mountain cat's neck.

He gathered Miranda against his body and felt for signs of life— any signs—with shifter magic. When he'd nearly given up hope, he found the faintest of heartbeats. Thank God she was still alive.

"Hang on, darling. My love, my mate."

Impossibly, the mountain cat growled low and menacingly. Its tail twitched weakly. *"I'll get her for this."*

Garen knew the words were for him. He didn't waste breath answering. He raised his 40mm semiautomatic Glock, aimed it at Alejandro's head, and fired at point-blank range. The report was loud in the enclosed space.

Lars burst into the hallway. "Jesus fucking Christ. It looks like a slaughterhouse."

Garen got to his feet, still holding Miranda's wolf form against his body. "I have to get her somewhere I can call lycan magic to heal her."

"I understand. The San Diego County Sheriff's office is on their way. I reported this location as a human trafficking compound."

"Good man." Garen hastened toward the stairs, grateful Lars had followed his part of the plan faithfully. "We need to be gone before they get here."

"Understood. One of the cars is out front, idling. I will drive you."

"The rest of the team?"

"They chucked the office computers into the hall where the cops will fall over them. Even if some officers have been protecting this operation, surely a few will gather the hard drives as evidence. I am always impressed by your agents. It only took them minutes to break the locks and grab the computers. Next they gathered the handful of women and children who were still here. They are on their way to freedom."

"Perfect. The cops will free the rest."

Lars snorted. They'd reached the street, and he held the back door of the Lexus SUV open for Garen. "You know how it is, old friend. Some of them will not wish freedom. It is easier to be taken care of, no matter what the price." He slammed the door and got behind the wheel. "Where to?"

"Head east, out into the desert."

"How is she?"

"Alive—barely. She lost a lot of blood. Wouldn't surprise me if that bastard had poison beneath his claws."

"He would have to have stuffed it beneath his fingernails in human form. Not likely."

"All right. I'm overreacting." He tightened his hold on Miranda. God, she felt good in his arms. If he could just get her strong enough to shift back to human form, he could drive her to a hospital for a transfusion. "Hurry."

"I will do the best I can. I do not wish to be pulled over. There is no way to explain why we have a wolf in the back seat."

They drove for a while in silence. At first, Garen thought it was his imagination, but he probed deeper with his magic. Miranda was definitely weaker, although he didn't see how she could be too much weaker and still be on this side of the veil.

"I have to shift," he told Lars. "If I can't access my full lycan magic, she'll die."

"Do what you need to. I will drive until I find a deserted place. And then I will drive a few minutes more."

Garen laid Miranda across the seats. He ignored his clothes, hearing them rip as the transformation took him. It was awkward in a space designed for humans, but he stood in the footwell and licked her wounds while sending healing magic into her. Lycans healed more quickly in wolf form. He prayed he wasn't too late. He crooned to her as he worked. Maybe his voice would help call her back from where she wandered, perilously close to death.

He wasn't aware how much time passed before the car lurched to a stop. It had been rough going for a while, so he assumed they'd turned onto a four-wheel drive road. Lars came around and opened one of the back doors. He gathered Miranda into his arms and carried her a few feet from the car.

Garen was right behind them. *"Put her down."*

"Is she any stronger?" Lars asked.

"Maybe, but it could be wishful thinking on my part."

Lars stripped out of his clothes. In moments, his mountain cat padded around Miranda's still form, sniffing. *"I think I might be able to help."*

Garen hesitated. A primal part deep inside wanted him to be the one who saved Miranda. He and no other.

I'm being stupid. Neanderthal.

"Please, Lars. If you have magic to counteract whatever Alejandro did, use it."

Lars laved Miranda's wounds with his sandpapery tongue. She had deep gouges in her flanks. When he finished one side, Garen helped him roll her over to expose the other. The shoulder Garen had pried Alejandro's jaws from was bitten down to bone. Lars focused intently on it—so intently Garen felt the sizzle of his magic.

A small whine escaped Miranda's jaws, and then another. Garen's heart took wing. He licked her snout and face furiously and infused healing magic into her body. Her wolf form twitched weakly.

"It's all right, darling. Don't try to move. We'll take care of you."

Lars sat back on his haunches, looking pleased with himself. *"Miranda. Find your human form."*

"No—" Garen protested. *"It's too soon."*

"Trust me, old friend. There will not be a better time—or a second chance." Lars shifted and picked up his clothes. He dressed, never taking his gaze from Miranda.

Garen shifted. He held Miranda against him. Her form shimmered and half formed into a human before it paled, and sank back to being a wolf. After Miranda's third failed attempt to shift, he sent a frantic glance at Lars. "It's too soon. The transformation will kill her."

"If she does not find her human body, she will be locked in her current form forever."

"Ridiculous. I've never heard of—"

"Quiet. You understand your magic, but not mine. I will explain later. Focus on her. Lend her your strength. I will do the same."

Miranda's wolf writhed in Garen's arms. Each time she tried to come back and failed, a little piece of him died. It was painful to watch her struggle. He felt impotent and ready to smash Lars' face in. He would have let her rest, drink some water, maybe eat something—

"Now." Lars' voice held a sharp, desperate note. "Pour power into her now."

Garen did. He gave her everything he had. After one heart-wrenching moment when he was certain she'd sink back to her wolf form, the air brightened. When it cleared, she lay in his arms, human once again.

Her eyes flickered open. "Is it truly you?" she croaked. "Or am I dead?"

The quick, hot prick of tears stung his eyes. "You're not dead, sweetheart. Thank Christ. You'll be fine. We'll get you to a hospital. They'll get some IV antibiotics going and—"

"That might not be necessary," Lars broke in. "Here." He handed her a bottle of water. Garen supported her head so she could drink.

Miranda drained it. "Is there more? I'm still really thirsty." Lars handed her another bottle. She glanced from one to the other.

"Guess I couldn't be dead. Not if both of you are here." Her gaze moved beyond them. "Where are we?"

"Desert east of San Diego," Garen replied.

"What happened back at the compound?"

Garen couldn't help himself. He grinned. What a woman. "Just back from death's doorstep and the first thing you want to know about is the operation."

Her gaze softened. "No, the first thing I promised myself, if I made it through alive, was to tell you how much I love you."

"I believe I shall take a walk," Lars said. "You both could stand a bit of privacy."

Garen snugged his arm around her shoulder. "Funny, it's similar to a promise I made myself."

She leaned into him. "Me, first. When I thought I might die and never see you again, I realized you were way more important to me than my work. Um, it's not that I plan to be dead weight or anything, but maybe we could go out on maneuvers together. Sort of watch each other's backs and all. I don't ever want to be separated from you again." She sucked in a shuddery breath. "I love you. There. I said it."

"There are some things I need to tell you—or maybe even better, show you—before you decide to tie your star to mine. I haven't been totally honest. I'd planned to take you to a romantic little getaway in the San Juans for this, but it's too important to wait for a perfect setting. Just a second." He rose to his feet.

"Where are you going? Crap. I just told you I love you, and you're leaving?"

"Don't worry. I'll be right back." The car door opened and then closed again. He hunkered next to her and draped a blanket over her because she had to be cold. The night air had a chill bite to it. He handed her a penlight.

"What's this for?"

"There's some moonlight, but I want you to take a really good look at me."

She struggled to a sitting position and pulled the blanket around her shoulders. "Thanks. Guess my clothes are in shreds beneath all that blood in the third floor hallway." She shivered. "Damn, but tonight was close. At least I killed him."

"No. He was still alive when I got there."

Miranda laid a hand on her chest. Shock bloomed on her face. "How is that possible? I severed his carotid with my teeth."

"Who knows? He's dead now. Shot him at point-blank range. I want to hear about tonight—every detail, but not just now. Look at me, Miranda. What do you see?"

Her gaze moved over his face and body. She shone the penlight and looked again. Her forehead creased. "Your eyes. They're not blue anymore."

"Perceptive, Miss Miller. Contact lenses can do amazing things." A corner of his mouth turned downward. Garen waited.

She shook her head. "It's hard to think. My brain feels like mush. Silver. Your eyes are silver. No one has silver eyes."

"Think again. Who have you—?"

Her muted shriek cut him off. She clapped a hand over her mouth. Her eyes widened, and the penlight fell into the sand, forgotten. "It can't be."

"Why not? You've seen me shift."

"Oh my God. You're Lucifer. And Garen. Ach, Christ. Don't mind me, I'm babbling." She pushed into his chest, knocking him onto his ass in the sand. He closed his arms around her and felt her tremble against him.

A small sob emerged, followed by another. "D-don't pay any attention to me. I'm just happy. The only two men I've ever wanted are one and the same. I can't believe it."

He arranged the blanket so it covered her back and rocked her against his body. "I guard my lycan identity. The only one who knows is Lars. And now, you. I love you, Miranda. I want to marry you just as soon as you're feeling up to it."

"Oh, my," she said around a hiccupy sob. "I accept."

"Not quite so fast, sweetheart. Not that I don't want you to say *yes*, but I have to tell you one more thing."

"What more could there possibly be?" She snaked her arms around his torso.

"I did you a tremendous wrong when I had sex with you in wolf form."

"I don't understand."

He sucked in a breath. "You will."

And I hope to God you'll forgive me.

"You may be too young to know this piece of lycan lore, but when one of us makes love with another in both our forms, we're bonded together forever. When we had sex over Ted's body, I sealed you to me even though it wasn't purposeful at the time. What I was trying to do was divert you, so you wouldn't discover I was the same wolf you'd seen outside the Index cabin."

"I'm still not understanding why it was so wrong."

"Maybe because I'm doing a piss-poor job of explaining. After we mated as wolves, it activated the shifter mate bond because we'd already had sex as humans. You could never love anyone but me, Miranda. If we weren't together, my thoughtlessness would've ruined your life."

She was silent so long his heart ached. "I'm sorry," he murmured against her hair. "I'll do whatever it takes to make it up to you." She shook her head against his chest, and he felt even worse. "Please, just give me a chance." He was groveling, but he didn't care. Miranda was his woman. He'd do anything to be able to love her and care for her and wake up next to her every morning for the rest of their lives.

She pulled away from him and met his gaze. "It's all right. I'm not angry, just overwhelmed. You didn't do it on purpose. I've been half in love with you for years, so moving my feelings from my heart to my body just made them deeper."

He'd opened his mouth to apologize more profusely. "What did you just say?" came out as a croak. He cleared his throat.

"That I love you. I want to marry you too."

"Are you sure? You can't work for me anymore."

"Maybe we could redo Rubicon International's incorporation articles. How about if we ran it jointly? Or even better, appoint a Board of Directors where we'd be two out of, say, half a dozen."

Christ! It's so simple. Why didn't I think of it?

Garen felt like an ass. "You know, it just might work. We could form a board from the most senior agents. Of course it would have to include people from Lars' European branch."

"You'll have to explain Rubicon's organization to me," Miranda murmured. "I know there are other offices, but—"

"Not if we're on the verge of changing it, I don't." Garen smiled warmly. "We can craft the new, improved RI as a group."

"Where there is a will…" Lars walked up next to them. "I assume there is peace in the kingdom."

"You mean queendom," Miranda said airily.

Garen snorted. "You could've stayed gone a little longer."

Lars shrugged. "Why? She is too weak to mate with right now. I saw no reason to march up and down the sand for another half hour. Bring her into the car. I will fire the engine, turn on the heat, and we will get something to eat. Miranda needs more than water to recover."

She laughed. It wasn't robust, but at least she was laughing. Garen's heart warmed with relief and gratitude.

"Awesome," she said. "Two of you to take care of me. A girl could get used to that."

"So long as his care stops at the bedroom door, we'll be fine," Garen growled. He got to his feet and helped her up.

"I take it that is your way of thanking me for helping to save your mate's life?" Lars' grin was visible even in the weak moonlight. Garen mock slugged him in the arm.

Miranda started toward the car. "Say, are there any clothes in the trunk? Two of us are naked."

"There should be." Lars popped the hatch and handed dark sweats around.

"My shoes are still in the back seat," Garen said. "Miranda doesn't have any, but it won't matter if we stop at a drive-in or carryout."

They settled inside the SUV. The heater warmed it quickly as Lars guided it back toward town. Miranda leaned against Garen. Her body felt wonderful. He reminded himself how close he'd come to losing her and kicked himself for being stubborn and shortsighted. He reached out with shifter magic, gratified Miranda's energy was recovering. She was much stronger than she'd been just a few minutes before.

"I guess I was really bad off when you found me," she murmured. "I passed out, and I don't remember anything until I woke up back there."

"Not dead, but not far away from it," Lars answered. "All cat shifters can produce venomous saliva. It creates a more-or-less permanent coma. We also carry the antidote, else our kind would have died out eons ago. All our young experiment with it—usually on one another."

"So that's what you did to bring her back," Garen mumbled half to himself. "I wondered."

"There is a window," Lars went on, "but it does not last very long. Once the antidote enters the bloodstream, the victim must find their human side. It breaks the enchantment."

"What if the victim's not a shifter?" Miranda asked.

"The venom kills them."

Miranda snuggled closer to Garen. "Alejandro said he knew me from Afghanistan."

Garen sucked in a breath. His stomach tightened. "So that bastard knew who you were before you came through his front door."

"It would seem so."

"If I'd realized that, I never would've—"

She twisted in his arms and laid a finger over his mouth. "Ssht. I'm here. You're here. If we engaged in Monday-morning quarterbacking, we'd never leave RI's headquarters."

"She is a smart one," Lars said and chuckled. "No wonder you fell in love with her. What does everyone feel like? Burgers? Asian? An early breakfast?"

"Yes." Miranda pounced on his last suggestion. "Let's do that. A Denver omelet and a cup of coffee would be perfect. There's one more thing before we get there, though."

"What might that be?" Garen asked, ready to face damn near anything with Miranda by his side.

"Alejandro could hear my telepathic speech when I was human. How is that possible?"

"He is one of the very old ones," Lars said. "Their magic was extremely strong."

Garen placed a hand on the side of her face and turned her to face him. "It's not easy, but turn your brain off for now. Concentrate on getting strong. There'll be plenty of time to dissect the operation. We don't need to do it now."

"Boss's orders?" she inquired archly.

"And mine," Lars seconded. "In case you were considering refusing. I see an IHOP ahead. Does that meet with everyone's approval?"

"Fine by me," Miranda relaxed against Garen. "I want buckets of coffee and an omelet and pancakes and—"

Garen kissed the top of her head. "Anything you want, darling. Anything at all."

EPILOGUE

hree weeks later

Miranda signed her name to what felt like the umpteenth document and then slid it to her right. Garen, Nadine, Jordan, and Lars were spaced around the oval table in Rubicon International's conference room. Two of Lars' agents had funneled in via webcam.

Brad Abernathy, the middle-aged, balding attorney Garen had hired to draw up new incorporation papers, said, "That's the last one, folks. I'll get these notarized as soon as you Heidelberg folk fax me your documents. Once that's done, send what I give you to the Washington State Department of Corporations. Until you get notice from them, your old articles are still in effect."

"How long does it usually take?" Garen asked.

The attorney shrugged. "Who knows with the government? If you don't have them in three weeks, give my office a call, and we'll see if we can't light a fire under them." He got to his feet and walked around the table gathering papers. His expensively tailored suit didn't have so much as a wrinkle, despite him sitting for over an hour.

Miranda glanced at her creased gabardine slacks and stifled a snort. Clothes had never mattered much to her. Work had been the most important thing in her life. Until Garen. She felt his gaze on her and smiled. The first week after her rescue had been hard. She'd wanted to do everything, but it took a few days to regain her full strength. Mostly, she'd wanted to lasso Garen into her bed and never let him loose, but he'd insisted on waiting until the doctor—that he demanded she see regardless of Lars' opinion—declared her well enough to return to normal activities.

"Bye, all." Brad stuffed papers into his expensive-looking leather briefcase and strode from the room. "I'll have these back in a couple of hours."

"Just slide them through the slot in the front door," Garen called after him. "We may not be here then."

"Got it."

"We will sign off for now," one of the Heidelberg agents said.

"*Ja*," the other concurred. "We must sign and fax so Herr Abernathy has what he needs."

"I will be back in Germany soon," Lars told them. "*Wiedersehen.*"

Amid a chorus of *Wiedersehens*, the wall screen shaded to gray.

"I would say this calls for a celebration." Lars went to an antique sideboard, the conference room's sole non-utilitarian piece of furniture, and picked up a bottle of champagne.

"I'll get glasses." Miranda rose and padded across the room on her flat-soled shoes. She set champagne flutes next to Lars and went back to her chair, waiting expectantly for the cork to pop. "Wahoo" and "Here's to us" filled the air as Lars caught most of the first rush of bubbly in a handy flute.

"We have an extra reason to celebrate." Garen looked meaningfully at Nadine and Jordan. "Lars already knows since he stood as my best man this morning at the courthouse, but Miranda is now my wife—and my mate."

Nadine's usually somber face broke into a grin. She vaulted from her chair, raced around the table, and bent to hug Miranda. "Wonderful news. Just wonderful. When I found out Alejandro was mixed up in the San Ysidro operation, I was plenty scared. If we'd known that before you went undercover, I would've argued against it."

Miranda got to her feet and hugged Nadine back. She let go and said, "Wow! I think that's the first time I've ever seen you smile. Thanks for your good wishes. Funny thing, but Garen said the same thing about Alejandro."

Jordan, who'd also gotten out of his seat, huffed. "It doesn't matter anymore. The bastard's dead, and that's all that counts. Hey, woman, move over." He hip-butted Nadine. "My turn to toast the bride—and kipe a hug."

It didn't take long before the champagne bottle was empty. Jordan stood behind Nadine's chair and tugged on it. "We need to go somewhere. Remember?"

"Huh?" Her confused expression smoothed. "Oh yeah. I'm on it. Right behind you." She picked up her small bag and got to her feet. "All the best. See you Monday."

"Now just a minute," Garen began and then stopped. "Okay, it is Thursday. I guess that's a not-so-subtle way of saying you're taking tomorrow off."

She shrugged. "It's not every day my boss gets married. I figured you'd want at least a little bit of a honeymoon." Nadine rolled her eyes at Miranda. "You'll have to work on him, sweetie. Get him to understand there's more to life than work."

Miranda's face split into a wide grin. "I plan to. Hate to admit it, but I've got the same problem. Overactive work ethic."

"Maybe we can help each other." Garen patted her arm.

Lars stood too. "I should get going as well. I am needed in Heidelberg."

"Anything we can do to help?" Garen got up and laid a hand on Lars' shoulder.

"I will let you know. It was a stroke of brilliance to solidify our business concerns with directors from both Heidelberg and Seattle. We shall be much more formidable."

"That was the idea. Since we were redoing the articles anyway, it was a natural extension. After all, we have common enemies."

Miranda watched them, a fond smile on her face. Like nearly every agent she'd known, Lars and Garen were tough people, men who dealt death for a living. Yet they understood tenderness as well. She hadn't forgotten Lars' pitch for her in the plane at JFK Airport. A thought blossomed. Maybe she could find him a woman. He had to be lonely. She knew how it felt because she'd been by herself for a long time before Garen captured her heart.

Miranda pushed to her feet and carried the glasses back to the small sink. She chucked the bottle in a trash can and turned to where the men chatted. "Thank you," she said to Lars. "You saved my life."

Color rose to his cheeks. He looked uncomfortable. "You are mate to my oldest friend. I could not have done less."

"Regardless. Thank you. I'm forever in your debt."

Lars cocked his head to one side and jabbed Garen. "Hear that? The lady owes me."

"Not that way, she doesn't. Don't you have a plane to catch?"

Lars glanced at his phone. "I shall be all right, but I do need to leave quite soon. Have you considered a European honeymoon?"

"What a grand idea." Miranda looked hopefully at Garen. "Paris, Venice, Rome."

"I'm sure we could find something to do in all those places," he agreed, a wicked grin on his face.

"How about just hopping from lush bed to lush bed?" She turned her best come-hither gaze his way.

"That does it. I am truly leaving now. Talk with you soon." Lars shouldered out the door.

"You don't have to go," Garen called after his departing back.

Lars stopped in the doorway and turned to face them. "*Ja*, but I do. Jaret Chen's heroin operation is out of control. I must see if I cannot institute measures to clip his wings."

"We'll help." Garen straightened his shoulders as he picked up the RI reins once again.

"Not until after at least forty-eight hours to ourselves," Miranda countered. "I want to touch and lick every single inch—"

"*Wiedersehen*! I will be in touch." Lars rolled his eyes, and the door closed behind him.

Garen laughed. "Hussy. You just drove my best friend out of here with all your sex talk."

"Like he hasn't heard it before. We need to find a woman for him."

"He used to say the same thing about me." Garen closed the distance between them and wrapped his arms around her. "What would you like to do with the rest of today? After all, it's not every day you get married."

She twined her arms around his back and tilted her head. He bent and kissed her, tenderly at first, and then more passionately as he sank his tongue deep into her mouth. His cock hardened against her stomach. She pressed against it and felt fluid dribble between her legs. Her nipples tingled with need. No matter how many times they made love, she couldn't get enough of him.

She broke away from their kiss. "I know. Let's go back to the room I had here."

"And then?"

"You're leering at me, Mister LeRochefort."

"You're my wife. I can leer all I want." He dropped his hands to her ass and pulled her firmly against his erection. "What happens after we get to your room?"

"We do it—twice. Once as wolves and again as humans."

He made a wonderfully male sound, possessive and savage, spun her about, and gave her a playful shove. "Just what I was about to suggest. Let's move out."

She laughed as she led the way out the door and up one flight of stairs to the apartment she'd stayed in. "Sheesh, you make everything sound like a field operation."

He slid an electronic key card from a pocket and opened the door. "You wish you had a field operations chief like me."

"Yeah, right. Bossy, overbearing. Hey, the door's not quite shut."

"Now it is. What were you saying about bossy? God, I love you to distraction, Miranda. You made me the happiest man alive by saying yes today. What do you want first, wolf sex or human?"

Instead of answering him with words, she slithered out of her clothes and reached for her wolf. A growl from behind told her he'd almost beat her to the draw. She turned so she could drink him in. *"You're the most beautiful wolf I've ever seen."* She licked his snout, and then took a step or two and shoved her head under his belly so she could lick his shaft, protruding from its furred sheath.

A panting growl filled the air. *"You're the beautiful one. Turn around, Miranda. You're driving me mad. I have to be inside you. Wolves don't do foreplay."*

Heat flared in her loins. Her tail twisted to the side of its own accord. Just to be a tease, she licked his cock twice more. Long, slow strokes. He nipped her back and then moved away from her questing mouth. His weight settled over her. His penis sank to the hilt, and the bulb at the base swelled, sealing them together. He rocked against her, pushing so deep she was certain he plumbed her very soul. Her muscles clenched around him and held tight as she came and came again.

Somewhere in the midst of her climaxes, he released inside her in juddery spasms that thrilled her. *"I love you, heart of my heart, soul of my soul,"* she murmured.

"And I love you, Miranda, dearest wife. Most wonderful mate." He nibbled her neck and turned his head to lick the side of her snout. She pushed her loins against him. He pushed back. After a while, the swelling at the base of his penis receded, and he pulled out of her. She rubbed snouts with him before reaching for her human form.

The air shimmered, and he stood before her, his eyes alight with love. The coppery tone of his skin gleamed in late afternoon sun slanting through the windows. "Would you like to clean up?"

"After the next round. And then you can buy me a wonderful, elaborate dinner with some hundred-year-old cabernet to go with Kobe steaks."

"Anything you want, darling."

She tossed back her head, laughed, and held out her arms. "I can't get a rise out of you. You were supposed to complain about the expense. You know me. I'm happy with Chinese takeout."

He gathered her close. "I'm happy with cardboard as long as you're next to me for the rest of our lives." He kissed her forehead and her eyelids before settling his mouth on hers. Slowly and inexorably, he backed her toward the bed and surfaced from their kiss. "I know we did it on the floor in this very room, but let's go for comfort. Neither of us is getting any younger."

She felt the bed against the backs of her knees and let herself fall across it. He followed her down. His mouth took up where it left off, and he strung kisses down her neck and breasts. Her nipples zinged with delight as he tongued first one and then the other. He sank a hand between her legs and rubbed her passion-slick clit. Her hips bucked, and her breathing quickened. Garen was an incredible lover. He got her so high, she thought she'd never settle back to earth.

She reached for him, but he batted her hands away and raised his head from her nipple. "Today is for you, darling. All for you. Tell me what you want. My mouth, my cock, my hands. All of them in a certain order."

"Wow. Like a menu. Maybe someday I won't be so hot I can't wait to get you inside me, but that day's not here yet. I want that—" she made another grab for his dick "—inside me. Now."

He grinned, repositioned himself, and licked her lips until she opened her mouth for his tongue. The head of his cock swirled around her opening, tantalizing all the hypersensitive nerve endings. She thrust upward, wanting to capture the glory of his amazing cock inside her, but he only gave her about an inch. He'd played this game with her before, and she loved it.

Her nails sank into his hips as she tugged, trying to get more of him inside. She locked her legs around his hips.

He moved his mouth away from hers and settled it over her ear. "Tell me." Whispery breath made shivers go up and down her back.

"Fuck me. I want all of you inside."

"With some men, this is all you'd get."

"I'm not married to some men. Did I tell you I married you for that amazing piece of equipment between your legs?" Her hips bucked.

"Not for my rapier-sharp mind? I'm crushed." More hot breath. More shivers.

"I love you," she panted. "All of you. Please. I'm going to come. I need you inside me."

He lowered himself, seemingly by centimeters, until at last he was all the way in. There was something so amazingly erotic about how he did it that by the time he hit bottom, she spasmed around him.

"Yes, darling," he crooned. "Come for me. That's it. Your nipples feel incredible, like hard little marbles against my chest."

He drew all the way out and slowly drove himself home. Another stroke and he groaned. She felt the tension in his ridged flesh deep within her and knew he rode a ragged edge of control. The game he played made him hotter than hell too. He'd told her often enough.

This time he stayed deep. Little, fluttery muscle movements drove her higher and higher. Her heart thrummed against her ribs. Her throat thickened with need, and her clit was on fire. Her breasts ached. "Yes," she breathed. "Harder. More. Now." She tightened her hands on his ass and got as close to him as she could. Her climax built, spooling from deep in her core, drowning her, shattering her.

His cock shuddered as her pussy convulsed around it.

He'd been supporting himself on his arms. His weight folded atop hers. For a time, they just held each other. "I'm happy," she whispered into the hollow of his throat. "So happy it scares me."

"I love you, Miranda. I'll take care of you. Nothing will ever threaten your happiness. Nothing."

He sounded so fierce, her lips curved into a smile. "What if I feel the same way about you?"

"I'll take it. Come on, sweetling. Let's shower and find something to eat. I liked your idea about a fine, oaky old cabernet and a tender steak, barely cooked."

"What are we waiting for?" She slid from beneath his body and headed for the bathroom. "I'm starved."

~

This is the end of *Garen*. Next book in the Rubicon International Series is *Lars*. Read on for a sample.

ABOUT THE AUTHOR

Ann Gimpel is a national bestselling author. A lifelong aficionado of the unusual, she began writing speculative fiction a few years ago. Since then her short fiction has appeared in a number of webzines and anthologies. Her longer books run the gamut from urban fantasy to paranormal romance. Once upon a time, she nurtured clients, now she nurtures dark, gritty fantasy stories that push hard against reality. When she's not writing, she's in the backcountry getting down and dirty with her camera. She's published over 50 books to date, with several more planned for 2018 and beyond. A husband, grown children, grandchildren and wolf hybrids round out her family.

Keep up with her at www.anngimpel.com or http://anngimpel.blogspot.com

If you enjoyed what you read, get in line for special offers and pre-release special reads. Sign up for Ann's newsletter on her website or her blog.

BOOK DESCRIPTION: LARS, RUBICON INTERNATIONAL, BOOK TWO

Tamara MacBride has a much bigger problem than hiding her shifter side from the world. By the skin of her teeth, and with a smattering of Irish luck, she manages to kill her sister's murderer. Escaping from the scene of the crime is much harder than she anticipated. Just when she thinks she might be safe, her cab driver shrieks and slumps over the wheel.

An unknown assailant terminates Lars Kinsvogel's target. Pleased by the outcome—after all dead is dead—he exchanges the glitz of Monto Carlo for a nearby airport intent on collecting the private plane he left there. He's no sooner arrived when a cab jumps the curb. His instincts blare a warning, but Lars ignores them and races over to investigate. There's not much he can do for the cabbie, but his passenger is still very much alive—and absolutely stunning. It takes some tall talking, but she agrees to come with him.

Espionage operations and runaway love travel halfway around the globe. Reticent to trust one another, it takes a series of crises and a near-fatal accident for them to take a chance on love—and each other.

LARS, CHAPTER ONE

*L*ars Kinsvogel sucked in an annoyed breath. Anxiety and greed thickened the air in Monte Carlo's Place de Casino, and he stifled a choking sound. Damn his hypersensitive shifter senses. If it weren't for them, the desperation hovering around him wouldn't be quite so palpable. Casinos were always like this, though, a haven for the rash and reckless. What had likely begun as a harmless pastime turned into hardcore addiction for an unfortunate few, forcing them to return again and again despite diminishing returns.

Hope springs eternal. All the poor sods need is one more spin of the wheel, another hand of cards... Lars glanced up, right into the croupier's beady gaze.

"Would monsieur like to place a bet?" The croupier grinned with all the warmth of a hammerhead shark, displaying a mouthful of bad teeth. What was it with the French and their aversion to dentistry? Lars shook his head and made shooing motions with one hand. He'd have to either join the baccarat game soon or move on, but he could get away with loitering for a few more minutes without drawing undue attention to himself.

His target, a powerfully built man with features revealing

Chinese ancestry, had an arm slung around a striking brunette. Maybe she was one of the hookers who worked the casino circuit, or maybe she was a steady thing for the man.

Lars considered it and decided she could be both. Around five feet eight, she had a lush, curvy body, dark hair cut into a stylish bob that fell a few inches past her shoulders, and memorable eyes the color of a restless ocean. A short, black sheath hugged her like a second skin. Open nearly to her waist, it displayed half her full breasts. Even though Lars' appraisal was surreptitious, he forced his gaze elsewhere. The woman was sex incarnate, and he didn't need anything diverting him from his objective.

Jaret Chen pressed chips into his companion's hand and urged her to pick a number. He gave one of her breasts a familiar squeeze, which earned him a smile, perfectly rouged lips stretching over impossibly straight teeth—and a slight shake of her head. Color stained her tanned skin. Lars realized he was looking at the woman again, wondering how her breasts would feel beneath his fingers. She seemed uncomfortable with Jaret's frank exploration of her body, so she probably wasn't a pro. For some unexplained reason, Lars felt relieved. The woman was too elegant to earn her living lying on her back.

He snorted to himself and studied the flashing display above the baccarat table. Maybe the woman wasn't French. That might explain her perfect teeth—and her discomfort with having her body mauled in public. At least she held Jaret's attention. So far the drug dealer hadn't spared him so much as a sidelong glance. Lars had never met the man, but knew a great deal about him from an extensive dossier provided by Rubicon International. Deeply involved in the heroin trade from the Middle East, across the Mediterranean, and into Europe, Jaret was one of the principals in a large operation—and Lars' current target.

He sized the man up. Maybe six feet, he had a barrel chest. Strongly muscled arms strained against the fabric of his cream-colored, silk dress shirt. His art deco tie had been loosened. Dark eyes, pronounced cheekbones, and straight dark hair cut short blended with his business attire. For all intents and purposes, he was indistinguishable from the phalanx of wealthy—and wannabe wealthy—men circulating through the casino. Lars glanced at his own cream-colored silk shirt and black linen pants. With the exception that his tie was still firmly knotted, he and Jaret were dressed as twins.

Guess neither of us wanted to stick out in anyone's memory.

Lars glanced at his Rolex. Close to midnight and time to move on. He'd seen enough. Now it was a matter of figuring out where and when to strike. These things always went more smoothly when he was close to invisible. He melted into the crowd and made his way outside. The casino fronted the French Riviera, and Lars stood looking out at the Mediterranean for long moments. The water was quiet tonight, waves barely slapping the white sand beach. His cell phone, set on silent, vibrated against his hip, and he tugged it from a pocket to look at the display.

Private. *Damn!* Could be anyone.

Lars punched the answer icon, held the phone to his ear, and waited. No need to say anything until he knew who was on the other end.

"Are you somewhere you can talk?"

Lars inhaled sharply as Garen LeRochefort's voice came through the phone's speaker.

Another shifter, Garen had founded Rubicon International with Lars hundreds of years before. The mechanics of the spy game had changed drastically between the late seventeen hundreds and modern times, but the basics—kill or be killed—hadn't altered much. Everyone who worked for Rubicon International was some type of shifter. Lars' animal form was a mountain lion, Garen's a wolf.

Lars loped farther down the beach until he cleared several couples engaged in deep, hungry kisses before responding. "What has happened?" Something must have, or Garen wouldn't have risked contact.

"You need to leave."

"But I have not—"

"Doesn't matter," Garen cut in. "I'll explain when you're back in the office on a fully encrypted line."

Lars thought about his twin engine Piper Seneca waiting at the Nice airport, twenty-four kilometers from Monte Carlo. It gave him freedom to come and go, and was much cheaper to operate than the business class jets he also owned. "Maybe I could still—"

"No!" The one word thundered so loud, Lars moved the phone away from his ear. "Don't even go back to your room." Garen hesitated. "Old friend. Trust me on this." The line went dead.

Lars stared at the iPhone's display and dropped the device back into his pocket. He'd been compromised. He wasn't certain quite how, and a part of him was curious as hell. He kept walking, swinging in a wide circle to head back toward the Hotel de Paris. Garen had said not to return to his room, but if he was careful, maybe he could learn something critical that would help their side.

"*Ja*, forewarned is forearmed," he muttered.

Keycard in hand, he let himself into a side door of the rambling old structure, got his bearings, and started cautiously up a stairwell. His suite was on the second floor, at the very end of the wing facing the Mediterranean. He'd always loved the old hotel with its thick, patterned carpets and antique lighting and furnishings. Staying next to the walls, he used a bit of shifter magic to cast a *don't look here* spell. It wouldn't keep someone determined from seeing him, but it didn't require much magic, either.

He entered the second floor a few doors from his own and scanned the empty hallway, his senses on high alert. Midnight was early in Monte Carlo, a city where people frequently stayed up through dawn and slept the day away, so he fully expected to see other guests, but the hall was mercifully empty. He padded silently toward his door and examined it, wishing he'd set a trap. He inhaled, trying to sort scents, but there were too many to make sense of. He could leave, just walk away like Garen had almost ordered him to, but Lars had never been a coward, and he was more intrigued than frightened. He'd spent years worming his way out of dicey situations. This was just one more, and he was damned if he'd walk away from his things. Not unless he had to.

He took a deep breath, tugged his guaranteed-not-to-set-off-metal-detectors .32 caliber revolver from its ankle holster, and shoved the key card into the slot in the door. A tiny electric motor hummed before the deadbolt snicked out of the way. He turned the latch, kicked the door open, and pivoted from side to side, scanning the sitting room of his suite, gun at the ready. Lars waited in the doorway, barely breathing, and then he heard a muted click, followed by an unmistakable whirr, and knew.

A bomb.

He cursed in German, not knowing if he was more annoyed with the turn of events or with himself for not taking Garen's advice and getting the hell out of there.

TAMARA MACBRIDE PUSHED the betting chips back into Jaret's hand. "Sure and I'm not feeling like wagering just now," she murmured. "Why don't you do it for me?"

He shot her an odd look. "But you like to gamble."

You only think I do.

"Something we had for supper didn't quite settle. Would you mind if I sat somewhere?" She swayed a bit on her feet to make her statement more realistic and sent a weak smile his way. In truth, she was a bit nauseated. Between sweat and greed, the air in the casino stank of humanity's darker side. Expensive colognes added a queer edge, their rich scents intensifying as their owners' anxiety rose. If she hadn't been a shifter, she might not have noticed, at least not as much. So far, she'd done a decent job hiding what she was from Jaret. She aimed to keep things that way.

He ran a thick index finger down the bare skin between her breasts. "We could return to our rooms."

She crinkled her face in what she hoped looked like an apology and did her best to ooze regret. "Better wait until my tummy settles." He was arrogant enough, he had no idea how repulsive she found him. Thank all the bloody saints, she'd managed to keep any sexual activities between them tamped down to nothing because of his heroin habit. According to a bit of Internet research, she supposed he could probably get hard, but the drug suppressed orgasms. At least so far, he'd been much more interested in his next shot of dope and drifting into an opiate-induced dreamy void than in bothering her for sex.

Jaret returned his attention to the baccarat table. "I'll just be over there." She pointed to a row of padded Louis Fourteenth chairs with bowed legs. Jaret nodded absently. His pupils were very small, so he was still fully under the influence of his last shot. That meant she had at least a couple of hours before he'd need to leave the casino.

Tamara tottered to a chair on ridiculously high heels. They made her feet ache, but Jaret liked it when she dressed like a fancy woman and pleasing him was high on her list. She settled onto the plush seat and slipped her shoes off. A waiter stopped and arched an inquiring brow. Nodding pleasantly at him, she ordered club soda. Rubbing the bridge of her nose between two fingers, she made a grab for her courage. So far, her plan had gone off without a hitch. The only thing left was to finish things off.

The waiter handed her drink over, along with a bowl of salted nuts, and she set both on a nearby chair. The ebb and flow of noise in the crowded room eddied around her. A quick glance at Jaret reassured her that he was still deeply engrossed in gambling—his second favorite addiction, right after heroin. He didn't care much for women, other than as window dressing and so the other men would see him as some sort of stud.

Tamara sipped her fizzy water and pursed her lips together. It was a long way from Dublin to Monte Carlo, and she wouldn't be here if it weren't for her sister. She bit her lower lip. Poor Moira. Dead at twenty-five. The coroner's report had listed a drug overdose as the official cause of death, but Moira hadn't been an addict. Her only crime was falling in love with Jaret Chen. Tamara had no idea how her sister actually died, but she knew in her bones that Jaret was responsible. Maybe someone had held her down while injecting enough of the crap to kill her.

She also had no idea how her sister could've been taken in by the Asian drug cartel lead-man, but Moira had always been drawn to powerful men. It was the only explanation.

She drained half her water and chewed a handful of cashews. Their entire family had been devastated by Moira's death, particularly her da. Tamara could still see his swollen, blotchy face at the funeral as he and three of her four brothers lowered the casket into the earth. The glass in her hand made an odd noise. She set it down before she broke it by accident. Moira had been a cat shifter, just like Tamara. Why the hell hadn't she claimed her animal form and killed the son of a bitch bent over the gaming table?

I'll never know.

She unclenched her jaw before her teeth cracked. She'd waited a few months so Jaret wouldn't be suspicious, and then searched him out. When he'd made a comment in passing that his last girlfriend had been Irish and had the same last name, she'd shrugged and blessed every goddess in the Celtic pantheon that Moira had the good sense not to tell Jaret anything about her family.

"MacBride's a common enough name in Scotland and Ireland," she'd informed him with a coy look, before asking, "What happened to her?"

"Who?" He'd looked the soul of innocence, the bastard.

"Sure and you know, your last girl pal. I'd hate to think she might come back to claim you." Tamara had held her breath then, torn between not wanting to hear whatever lie he came up with and being desperate for information.

He'd shrugged. "Hard to say quite what happened. Guess she dumped me." He'd made a sour face and muttered something disparaging about women under his breath.

That had been two months ago. In the intervening time, she'd inveigled her way into his life. Because she was attractive, pleasant, and never made any demands—easy enough since she couldn't bear the sight, or stench, of him—he'd allowed her into his inner circle.

She closed her teeth over her lower lip. The only thing she hadn't done was kill him. It would be easy enough. He slept like a dead thing because of his drug habit. She could do the deed and be out of their bedroom and on her way hours before anyone discovered his body. She'd never formally registered as a hotel guest. Jaret had his reasons for wanting her invisible. Apparently, he'd never guessed she might have her own.

So why haven't I finished this?

The answer bubbled up, and it sickened her. Nothing in her chosen profession as a freelance photojournalist had prepared her for wholesale slaughter. She was a coward, plain and simple. Killing in her mountain lion form was one thing. It felt...natural. Not that she'd ever killed anything except game to eat, even shifted. To take a life, in a cold-blooded, carefully thought out manner, repelled her. She'd dreamed of shoving her knife into Jaret's carotid, even circled him while he slept, blade in hand, but in the end she hadn't been able to force herself to strike.

Her hands ached because she'd balled them into fists. Once she uncrimped her fingers, blood welled where her nails had sliced into her palms.

Either I do this thing, or I need to leave.

An unpleasant thought surfaced. She was in so deep, he'd never just let her walk away. Maybe that had been Moira's undoing. Sick to death of playing third fiddle behind Jaret's addictions, maybe her proud sister had issued an ultimatum and ended up with enough heroin in her bloodstream to kill a moose.

The more she considered it, the more certain Tamara was she'd hit within spitting distance of the truth. She gazed at her lap and pulled the gaping front of her dress closer together. There wasn't any choice. Not really. He'd never let her go, so she had to latch onto enough moxie to finish him off.

"Another drink, mademoiselle?" The waiter was back. He stared at her half-exposed breasts, a lascivious grin not far from the surface.

She nodded. "Scotch. Single malt. Twenty years old, or more."

"Very good, mademoiselle. Anything to go with it?"

What could she order that wouldn't blow her upset stomach story? "Um, crackers, with some brie."

The waiter walked away. She stared after him. In a very distant way, he looked like the Teutonic god who'd been eyeing them from across the baccarat table earlier. The tall, blond man had been broad-shouldered and slim-hipped. His eyes were a cool, icy gray, and his facial bones damn near perfect, with a square jaw and pronounced cheekbones. He hadn't smiled, but she imagined his teeth would be very straight.

Why can't I have someone like that in my life?

Because I'm a shifter, goddammit. It's a big secret to keep.

Yeah, and to keep on keeping it made her weary. She'd given up on a normal life when the first change came on her shortly after she hit puberty. There were laws to ensure shifters didn't get out of hand that included killing them—or shipping them off to prison. It was prudent—and necessary—to hide what she was, rather than embrace it. Her parents, both shifters themselves, had hammered that point home until she was sick of hearing it.

The waiter had just stopped by with her drink and crackers with cheese when Jaret joined her. "Feeling better, I see." He pried the glass from her hand, swallowed half its contents, and raised his eyebrows. "Expensive."

"I can pay for it. I still have a little money."

He rolled his eyes. "No, no. Wouldn't dream of that. You're my woman, aren't you?" At her pleasant nod, he went on, "I take care of my women. Good care of them. Come on." He tugged her to her feet.

"Wait. My shoes." She bent and fished them from beneath her chair. Hanging onto him, she balanced first on one foot, then the other, while she slid her feet into the pumps. "Okay." She grinned broadly. "All ready."

"Do you want to bring the crackers along?"

"Sure. Why not?" She gripped the plate in one hand and curved the other around his arm. He finished her drink and steered them out of the casino toward the stairs that led to the Hotel de Paris.

Tonight, she told herself. *Before tonight's over, he'll be dead. Moira can rest in peace, and I'll be out of here.*